MONSTER BELOW

The seawater outside the *Helldiver* became the color of the ink squirted by a frightened octopus.

"My God!" Ham breathed. "If there *is* such a creature . . ."

"Doc," Johnny said wonderingly. "Do you remember the legends of the Kraken—a giant devilfish who would ensnare whole ships with his tentacles? It was said he slept for centuries between each attack, and that one day he would wake up for good and bring the world to an end."

The *Helldiver* gave a violent shake, as if it were a bone grabbed by a very large dog. They were thrown about the inside.

A crunching roar assailed their ears.

"It's attacking!" Ham screeched. . . .

The New Adventures of Doc Savage
Ask your bookseller for the books you have missed.

ESCAPE FROM LOKI by Philip Jose Farmer
PYTHON ISLE
WHITE EYES
THE FRIGHTENED FISH

(*Don't miss another original Doc Savage adventure*, THE JADE OGRE coming in October 1992)

THE FRIGHTENED
FISH

Kenneth Robeson

BANTAM BOOKS
NEW YORK · TORONTO · LONDON · SYDNEY · AUCKLAND

THE FRIGHTENED FISH

A Bantam Falcon Book / July 1992

Interior Art by Joe DeVito.

ISBN 0-553-29748-1

Published simultaneously in the United States and Canada

PRINTED IN THE UNITED STATES OF AMERICA

OPM   0 9 8 7 6 5 4 3 2 1

DOC

Doc Savage—born Clark Savage, Jr.—was raised from the cradle for his task in life—his job of flitting about the globe righting wrongs, helping the oppressed, smashing the guilty. He is a physician and surgeon—and a mighty good one, the tops in his line. He has the best and most modern equipment at his command, for he has limitless wealth. His main headquarters are in New York, but he has his Fortress of Solitude at a place unknown to anyone, where he goes at periodic intervals to increase his knowledge and concentrate. He's foiled countless crooks, and changed many of them into honest, useful citizens. The world would be a great place if there were more Doc Savages. But there's only one.

HAM

You'd never think a gentleman named Brigadier General Theodore Marley Brooks would be called Ham—would you? But Monk, Ham's pal, had a reason for giving him the nickname. He thought it would irritate the dapper Brigadier General Brooks—and that alone was regarded as a good reason by Monk. Ham is a knockout dresser and a knockout fighter, too. There's very little of the law that he doesn't know down to about six decimal places. But in a fight, the main law that he thinks about is the law of self-preservation, although most of his battles have been in the interest of folks too weak to fight for themselves. His slender black swordcane is something to avoid.

MONK

When you look at this picture, you can understand
very well why the subject is called Monk. Hardly any
other nickname would fit him as well. He's a tough
hombre. His arms are six inches longer than his legs,
and with this gorilla build he seldom stacks up against
any opponent who's more than a brief workout for him.
No one ever calls him by his real name of Andrew
Blodgett Mayfair. And maybe they'd better not! There's
a ring to it that Monk might not like! Yet Monk has a
keen brain as well as a strong body, and is reputed to be
one of the world's greatest chemists. His combination of
body and brain makes him a big asset to Doc Savage's
intrepid little band of crusaders.

RENNY

If you know him well, you can call him Renny. If you want to be formal, it's Colonel John Renwick. He's a giant of a man. A six-footer would have to look up at him. He weighs well over two hundred, and while he doesn't throw his weight around, he knows how to use it in a fight.

His fists—and they are very big and bony—are very bad on faces. They can actually shatter the solid panel of a heavy door. Renny is an engineer, and tops in his line.

LONG TOM

Major Thomas J. Roberts—Long Tom to his friends—is the electrical wizard of Doc Savage's little group of adventurers. In spite of his nickname, he is not so tall. Doesn't weigh so much, either, and the appearance of his skin gives the impression that he might not be in the best of health.

That skin, however, has been misleading to anybody who ever picked on Long Tom for a set-up. Try taking a cougar's cubs away, but don't ever shove around Long Tom. He's as fast as light, and a terrific socker.

JOHNNY

Few persons would take Johnny—whose real name is
William Harper Littlejohn—for a scrapper. He's quite
studious. He's an archæologist of worldwide reputation.

Anybody who picked up Johnny, however, would
be making quite a big mistake. He can fight like a
wounded panther when he's aroused. Like a great
many gaunt men, he has an inexhaustible reservoir of
strength. He's an important member of Doc Savage's
little group.

PAT

Pat Savage is a cousin to the man of bronze. She has Doc's metallic coloring—bronze skin, flake-gold eyes— and is extremely attractive. Pat operates one of New York's most exclusive beauty salons, and constantly yearns for excitement. Though highly capable, her participation in the adventures of Doc and his aides is usually against Doc's wishes, for he believes the work of his group too dangerous for a girl.

Contents

I

FEAR OF FISH

The man was tall, with sand for hair and a hide whose raw color and abraded roughness suggested that he had spent much time around the sea. The tips of his sunburned ears were red and peeling in spots. He was an ordinary man except for one particular: Fear rode his rubbed-by-sandpaper features, twisting them with unnerving harshness.

It was that harshness of expression which made the headwaiter of the restaurant nervous as he conducted the man to a corner table by the window. The sunburned man had specifically asked for that table in a tense voice. His tone added to the headwaiter's unease. After ascertaining that the man didn't desire a cocktail, the headwaiter hurried off, leaving him to peruse his menu in tight silence.

The restaurant was one of those peculiar establishments that can be found in Greenwich Village. Innocuous on the outside, it was decorated with disquieting gaudiness within. It was the lunch hour, but the restaurant wasn't crowded. One table over from the sunburned one with sand-colored hair, three men sat huddled in earnest conversation. They looked like typical New York businessmen, which made them overdressed for the casual Bohemian atmosphere.

Presently, a waiter—it was the table waiter—rolled an aquarium up to the table where the three businessmen sat. He presented each customer with a pair of tongs, which they employed to extract the fish of their choice from the tank. One man had some difficulty snaring his intended meal—a butterfish—causing him to remark aloud, "I'm not so sure I like this any better than ordering from a menu. I can't seem to trap the little beggar."

"At least you can be sure that you're eating fresh fish," a companion laughed.

That last comment caused the sunburned man seated nearby to look up from his menu in shock. His shock turned to near-panic when he saw the man finally tong a flat silver fish from the portable water tank.

"No! No!" he screeched. He bolted to his feet, upsetting his table. "Take it away!"

"Here, now, fellow. What is this?" the man with the fish demanded. It squirmed and flopped between the tongs, its gill flaps fluttering with delicate urgency.

The sunburned one, a picture of utter and complete panic, tried to run. He tripped over his own chair. The commotion caused patrons all over the restaurant to stand up and gawk. The trio at the water tank followed suit. One of them, still clutching his tongs tightly, made a move to offer his free hand to the fallen customer. As he leaned down to help, the flopping silver fish eeled from the loosening tongs. It landed on the agitated man's chest.

The man's eyes riveted on the fish, now in the final convulsions of death. With a last weak squirm, it lay flat. Only its puckered mouth worked after that.

"Take it away! Take it away!" the sunburned man bleated, his eyes pleading. "I can't stand the look of fear in its eyes!"

"It's all right, friend," the helpful man said soothingly

as he tonged the fish up, leaving a damp smear on the prostrate man's shirtfront. He brought it up to the other's nose. "See, it won't harm you."

Instead of producing the expected calming effect, the gesture had the opposite result. In a frenzy, the sunburned individual grabbed from the floor the knife which had bounced from his overturned table setting, and jumping back into a corner, applied it to his own throat.

"Hey! That guy's trying to kill himself!" one of the three businessmen yelled.

"Somebody stop him!" another howled. "No, I'll do it." He jumped the man, who was sobbing horribly, but otherwise accomplishing little. A bread knife is not quite the instrument with which to cut one's own throat.

There was a brief tussle, with the result that the would-be suicide landed back on the floor, the victim of a judo throw.

The man who had done the throwing stepped back and asked of the gaping restaurant clientele, "Did you see that! He tried to kill himself when he saw me pick out that silver fish! Why would anyone be frightened of a little silver fish?"

The silver fish in question, meanwhile, gasped for air on the floor, but no one paid it any attention, and it died there. In death, it wore a scared, round-eyed expression not unlike that of the man who had been terrified by it.

The would-be suicide found his feet momentarily. He looked dazed. He ran one shaking hand through his shock of sandy hair. No one tried to stop him when he stumbled from the restaurant like a hagridden old man.

The other patrons slowly resumed their seats. The waiters busied themselves with their duties, deflecting questions with bored shrugs and murmurs.

Not long after, the three businessmen filed out of the restaurant without a word, their meal forgotten.

An hour later, the same sunburned man walked down a lower Manhattan side street near the Battery, his face warped with ugly tension. His progress appeared aimless until he came abreast of a run-down corner market. There was a large fish in the window, lying on its side in a tray of ice. The fish was silver. Even its flat dead eye was silvery. The eye looked uneasy, as if even in death it feared its eventual fate.

The man noticed it with a stride-stopping start. He panicked again. He screamed. High and shrill, the sound was something to chill the bone marrow. It attracted attention up and down the street. People came out of doorways and leaped from passing cars. A few converged on the sound.

"They're everywhere!" he shrieked. "The frightened fish are everywhere! I can't escape them! No one can escape them!"

The man looked around wildly. He spied an approaching taxi. He started toward it, and his intention to hurl himself in the path of the machine became obvious to passersby.

Two men jumped him before he got twenty feet. The taxi braked hard, slowed, and struck a lamp post. The impact banged the cab's grille out of shape, but the driver emerged unscathed.

"What the blankety-blank is going on?" the cabby demanded, not using quite those words.

One of the rescuers yelled back, "I don't know, dammit! This guy lyin' here took one look at a fish in that market window and went crazy. I think he was tryin' to get himself run over."

The man in question lay dazed in the street. A bewildered crowd gathered.

"What's so damn terrifying about a fish?" the cabby wanted to know.

"Nothin' that I can see," the second rescuer put in. "It's just a fish, a common silver carp. Looks more scared than that guy, you ask me."

They went over to the window to look at the fish. The whole street went over to the window. Some squeezed into the tiny market itself, causing the proprietor to have fits. No one was buying.

While all this attention was being focused on a storefront fish, the one with the suicidal inclinations picked himself up and ran off.

A few minutes later, his two rescuers entered the slightly damaged taxi. The cabby was already behind the wheel. He drove off. Not a word passed between them.

The Parkside-Regent Hotel, overlooking Central Park, was quiet as three well-dressed men entered the lobby, ostensibly to secure rooms for themselves. They wore overcoats and carried luggage, which made them look like out-of-town visitors.

They were the same three men who had tried to prevent the suicide of the man who had been fright-, ened by a fish in a Greenwich Village restaurant earlier in the day. Dressed differently, they were also the same trio who had been involved with the near-suicide in front of a Battery market. One of them had been driving the taxi. They were preoccupied now with details of registering at the Parkside-Regent.

They didn't appear to notice that the man with the ungodly fear of fish had quietly entered the lobby to purchase a newspaper from a cigar stand. He paused at a rack of postcards, casually turning the spinner to examine the display.

Abruptly, he let out a howl that produced a sympathetic squeal of fright from the counter girl. He knocked the card-spinner to the floor. His eyes were wild. He kicked at the fallen rack as if it were a vicious dog. Cards scattered all over the floor. Several of these fell faceup to reveal the picture of a mounted swordfish. The swordfish was silver. Its profile suggested wide-eyed, gape-mouthed terror.

The sight brought renewed screams from the man, and from the counter girl. The man stamped at the postcards frantically, but to no avail. "Get them away! *Get them away from me!*" he wailed. "They haunt my dreams, those frightened fish!"

He ran then. Not for the revolving door, which was clogged with a matron pulling a small dog on a leash, but for a big plate-glass hotel window. Head lowered, he butted the pane like an enraged bull. The glass was stout. He bounced back. Sobbing, he then picked himself up to try again. He bounced a second time, which brought tears of frustration to his eyes, but no willingness to give up. His object, it was plain, was to dash his brains out against the glass. But he was unable to build up enough of a head of steam to complete the task. It was a horrendous sight.

The three men at the lobby desk went into their act—it was not obviously an act to bystanders—once again. Yelling, they piled on the other man before he could smash his skull against the lobby window a third time. They wrestled him to the ground as the manager frantically called the police.

By the time the police arrived, minutes later, the suicidal man had vanished. So had his rescuers. The manager, who was almost entirely speechless, professed to understand none of it.

The counter girl, considerably calmed down now, gave her version of what happened.

"He didn't act crazy, at first," she explained, chewing

gum nervously. "He came in, bought a paper, and started looking through the postcards. Then, well, he just turned into a maniac. Fella destroyed the rack for no reason."

That much was obvious to the two cops. "Did he say anything?" one asked.

The girl thought. "It was mostly yelling, but he did say something about fish haunting him, or something like that. I remember him stamping on the ground like a crazy man. You know, kinda the way you'd step on a poisonous snake. Except I didn't see any snake. Just postcards."

The two cops looked over the rug. They found several postcards scattered about, all bent and scuffed, and all bearing the identical photograph of a mounted swordfish. There were other postcards strewn on the rug, the usual Manhattan skyline portraits intended for the tourist trade, but these were undamaged.

"This is screwy," one of the cops remarked, puzzled.

"It sure is. Why would he be scared of a swordfish?"

"You ask me, the swordfish looks darned unhappy, too."

"I never heard of a scared swordfish," the second cop remarked.

"Well, we'd better call the boys at Bellevue. Could be one of their inmates is loose."

"An escaped lunatic. Sure, I'll bet that's who he was."

They left the hotel with their shared opinion unchanged.

The skyscraper was New York's tallest. For that matter, it was the tallest in the world. It rammed up from the pavement over one hundred stories in height from its busy modernistic lobby to the needle point of its dirigible mooring mast—a ludicrous adornment in an age of jet aircraft. It boasted more offices than some small cities. The skyscraper was famous for another reason, too. Its eighty-sixth floor was the headquarters of Doc Savage, an individual whose avowed profession was no less Galahadian than that of righting the wrongs of the world and bringing malefactors to justice, where normal law-enforcement agencies could not do so.

Almost everyone—including Doc's enemies, who were many—knew of Doc Savage and his work, and knew also, that he operated out of this midtown Manhattan skyscraper. That was why the elevator operators in the building received instructions to report any unusual occurrences in the busy lobby.

Doc Savage was in his laboratory—his suite consisted of a laboratory-library-reception room set-up—when the phone rang.

"Mr. Savage? This is Henry, one of the elevator operators."

"Go ahead, Henry." Doc's voice was quietly powerful, like the engine of an expensive limousine as it idles.

"There's somethin' funny goin' on down here you might want to know about."

Interest lifted the controlled timbre of Doc's tone. "What is it?"

"There's these three guys hangin' around out front."

"Describe them."

Henry did so. The descriptions meant nothing to Doc Savage.

"Continue, Henry."

"Well, they were just hangin' around, like I say, but as soon as they thought no one was lookin', they got down and drew a fish on the sidewalk."

"A fish?"

"I know how it sounds, but that's what they did. I watched them from the lobby. They drew a fish outline in chalk. I think it's a porcupine fish."

"What's unusual about that?" Doc asked. "College pranksters perpetrate these sorts of stunts every day."

"That's my point," Henry said excitedly. "These guys weren't frat boys. None of them looked under thirty. After they drew the outline, they filled it in with silvery paint."

"What did these men do after that, Henry?"

"They ducked around the corner. They're still there, too. Like they're waiting for something to happen. But don't ask me what."

"Anything else to report?"

"Yes. I don't know who looked more frightened, them or the fish."

"Eh?"

"The fish," Henry said, "is wearing the most terrified expression you ever saw."

"Thank you, Henry," Doc Savage said after a pause. "You did the right thing to call." He hung up.

The information had both puzzled and intrigued Doc Savage. The altercation involving the man whose fish phobia was so great that he would try to take his life had made the afternoon editions, and Doc had read an account of the matter. He had thought little of it until a television news broadcast of the incident at the Battery market came over the air. The Parkside-Regent incident was too recent for him to have heard about.

Swiftly, Doc shucked off a laboratory smock discolored by the chemicals of an experiment he had been performing on the molecular stability of polymers. He strode across the huge laboratory.

Doc Savage was a spectacular man. He had a reputation as a combination scientific genius, mental marvel, and physical giant, which he more than lived up to. He lived up to his reputation, as a matter of fact, the way the atom bomb lives up to its reputation as an explosive weapon. In person, Doc was a giant bronze

man with hair a little darker than his skin, and a pair of
compelling flake-gold eyes that could calm you down or
lift you out of your seat—whichever effect Doc desired.
He was a man of immense physical strength whose
intelligent face ended any suspicion that he might be all
muscle and no brain. It was a face whose handsomeness
was made tolerable, to Doc's way of thinking, by its
angular regularity.

All in all, the giant bronze man was too conspicu-
ous to investigate the mystery of the fish-drawing pranksters without taking precautions. Doc was a genius at
taking precautions. Truth to tell, he was a genius at
most of what he did.

Doc dug a cab driver's uniform and cap out of a
clothes locker, changed into it, and took his special
pneumatic elevator to the secret garage he maintained
in the skyscraper's basement. There, he left the establishment in an old taxi, exiting through a secret door
activated by a radio signal from the cab, which happened
to be bullet-proof, among other not-very-obvious wonders.

Doc turned the corner, spotted three men answering
the elevator operator's description loitering by a telephone booth, and hit a dashboard button. The left front
tire in the cab let go like a shot. The car veered wildly.
Making a show of the struggle, Doc fought the wheel to
the curb opposite the three men. He got out and
proceeded to go through the motions of changing the
tire, seeming not to pay any attention to the loitering
trio.

The three men were huddled in conversation. The
two doing most of the conversing more or less faced
Doc, which was fortunate because it enabled him to
read their lips with a gadget consisting of a mirror
attached to a telescopic rod, somewhat like the examining tool dentists use. Doc was a skilled lip-reader.

"This is ridiculous," one of the trio was saying. "Here we are practically camped on his doorstep. And who says this goofy stunt is even going to work?"

"I don't hear any better suggestions," growled the other. He possessed a hard, weather-beaten face with light-colored eyes that brought to mind carpet tacks. There was absolutely no warmth in them. "And where the hell is George? I told him two o'clock. It's ten past."

"I'm more worried about Savage, dammit. He's big stuff."

"So is this, brother," the second speaker said fervently. "So is this."

"I keep hearing that, but I still don't see how any of these fish shenanigans are going—"

"What do you want we should do?" the second man—he seemed to be the group's leader—remarked with strained exasperation. "Go up there and ask him? 'Excuse us, Mr. Savage, but we're with Max Wood's outfit, and we were wondering, before we get too deep into our activities, whether or not you have been warned about us and intend to put a stop to these activities?' Is that what you want us to do? Is it?"

The first man shifted his feet. He rolled a well-chewed toothpick from one side of his mouth to the other. All three were watching the street, searching approaching faces.

"But this fish thing is screwy—"

"Sure, but if Savage knows anything, he'll be getting ready to tear off for Quincy. We have to find out now and head him off. He's the only one who could queer the whole plan. He's exactly the type, too; this is just his damn meat." The man stepped away from the others and peered around the corner toward the skyscraper's main entrance. Seeing nothing more than the usual New York pedestrians unconcernedly trampling the silver-paint sidewalk fish, he returned to the others.

"Now, we've pulled this scared-fish gag in enough places all over town to get his attention, but he hasn't made a move so far. One last try in front of his headquarters should do it. He'll grab George. George will tell him a fable and pump him. And there you have it. We either skrag Savage or make tracks, depending on how close to being a monkey wrench in our well-oiled works he is."

The third man, away from the mirror, suddenly pointed north toward a man crossing the street.

"Here comes that damn George now," the straw boss muttered without pleasure.

"About damn time."

They gathered themselves into a close-knit knot, straightened out their clothing as if it would smooth out the nervous lines of their faces as well, and turned the corner, the straw boss man taking the lead.

Doc, on the opposite sidewalk, abandoned his flat tire and took up a position in a phone booth where he could better keep an eye on the others.

A sunburned man with sandy hair and a grim face was striding toward them, Doc saw. He did not appear to recognize the trio, nor notice the spiny silver fish on the concrete until he stepped on it. Then he definitely took notice of the design.

His head went down. His face went slack.

He leaped a foot in the air and his blood-curdling yell bounced along the street. "The fish!" he screeched. "The frightened fish! It means the end of civilization!" He began pulling at his hair. He beat his chest, his head, his sides, and presented a convincing portrait of a demented and terrified person.

The trio, acting the part of bystanders, fell upon him, wrestling him to the ground, and otherwise made a big show of protecting the screaming man from himself. They eyed the skyscraper entrance at every opportunity.

Doc Savage walked up from the opposite side of the street.

"You can cut the acting," Doc told them all.

One of the trio looked up in bewilderment. "What—what did you say?" he gulped.

Doc removed his driver's cap. "I said you can drop the act," he repeated. "I know everything." Nothing on his face indicated this last was a fib.

Open-mouthed astonishment transfixed the quartet of men, a tangle of bodies on the sidewalk.

"You do?" one spoke in a hoarse croak. It was the sunburned newcomer. George.

"I do," Doc told him.

"Then I guess it's all over," George muttered, staring down at the spiny sidewalk fish that looked as if it were frozen in terror.

Then one of the men pulled a pistol and shot the bronze man twice.

Doc Savage was driven backward three steps by the force of the bullets. He kept his feet, as if fighting to hold onto his balance against a hurricane-force gale, not a sudden flurry of .38-caliber slugs. With the third step, he twisted at the knees and ankles and collapsed on the curb. He did not rise again.

The quartet of men took off in a flock, knocking through the gathering crowd like football linemen. A waiting car carried them away.

Doc Savage picked himself up. His breathing was red agony. Both bullets had hit him in the solar plexus, a particularly bad spot, even with the bullet-proof chain mesh undershirt protecting it. He fought for air, as he shook off the solicitous hands of the gathering crowd. He made for his cab.

A press of a dashboard button reinflated the supposedly flat tire, and the cab got under way.

Doc caught sight of the fleeing car almost immediately, reasoned out its general direction, and kept abreast of it by running down parallel streets on either side. Manhattan's gridlike street layout made this simple. Meanwhile, he concentrated on getting his wind back and mentally berated himself for allowing himself to be shot. The zaniness of the man-terrified-by-frightened-fish lure had caused him to underestimate his opponents.

The trail led north to the Queensboro Bridge and then to Long Island. Doc was calculating his best next move—whether to follow at a distance or cut his quarry off and confront them—when they turned onto an abandoned flying field near Patchogue, and he knew with a sinking certainty that the quartet of suspicious men would have had a plane standing by for just such an eventuality as this.

He was right. Floats bumping along the rutted, weed-choked ground, a small yellow seaplane took off moments later and moaned northward.

Doc Savage watched it with unwavering metallic concern etched on his bronze mask of a face.

II

MYSTERY CONCERNING FISH

Monk Mayfair was waiting when Doc Savage returned to his headquarters reception room. Monk was Lieutenant Colonel Andrew Blodgett Mayfair, one of Doc Savage's five associates and one of the world's great industrial chemists, although he hardly looked the part. He was a short, wide man with the knots-of-muscles physique and general disposition of a bull ape.

Monk had his fingers in his ears in an attempt to shut out the noisy shouting emanating from the next room, the library. It was quite a row, from the sound of it.

"What now?" Doc asked wearily. He was used to Monk's pranking enough to suspect some form of practical joke.

"Woman trouble," Monk said in a deceptively childlike squeak. His twinkling pig eyes popped open as he lowered his improbably long arms.

"Again?"

"Not me. Johnny. He just blew back into town, and me and Ham thought we'd all drop in, but you had gone. Next thing, this babe shows up, all hot under the collar and lookin' for you. Said you knew where her fiancé was, and she wanted him back pronto. Well, this spitfire didn't exactly cotton to your not being available.

15

She got even more wrathy. We tried to calm her down, but Johnny made the mistake of usin' some of his words on her. That *really* set her off—"

"Let's see about this," Doc said sharply. They marched into the library.

The girl was short and blonde, and five-eighths mouth, it seemed to the bronze man. She was saying: "I repeat, I'm Celia Adams of the Massachusetts Adamses and I can buy and sell the whole lot of you clowns. So if you don't tell me where Baker is—"

"An imponderability," said a long stringbean of a man who stood regarding the blonde through a handheld monocle as if she was some hitherto-unknown specimen of feminine evolution.

Celia Adams called the long stringbean an unladylike name, which caused the latter's face to color. He stepped back hastily. The eye behind the monocle swam.

"See here, now, miss." This was from a handsome individual who was decked out in striped trousers, dark swag coat, and fawn lap-over vest. He was formally known as Brigadier General Theodore Marley Brooks—otherwise "Ham" Brooks, noted attorney and Doc Savage aide. Unlike Johnny—William Harper Littlejohn—the long-worded archæologist, Ham considered himself something of a rake, but he wasn't doing too well with Celia Adams. He waved his dark cane excitedly. "That is no way for a lady to talk," he protested.

"Can the charm school lecture, you prissy-faced diplomat! I want Baker Eastland, and I want him *now!*"

Doc Savage cut off Monk's rude chortle. "Perhaps I can assist you, Miss Adams," he said. "I'm Doc Savage."

Celia Adams spun around. If the reputation or presence of the Man of Bronze—Doc was called that sometimes—impressed her, she gave no sign. Her tirade continued uninterrupted; she merely redirected it.

"Where is Baker?" she demanded with an attention-getting stamp of a well-shod foot. "He's been gone five days. I know he came here; he told me he was going to. And we are supposed to be married in a few days! This is *absurd!* And to top it all off, these . . . these *morons* of yours refuse to give me any satisfaction."

Doc waved an impatient hand. "Let's boil the meat off this bone of contention, shall we? You say you are Celia Adams and your fiancé, Baker Eastland, has vanished after telling you he intended to seek me out. Is that much correct?"

"Yes." Celia stamped her other foot this time. "And I demand—"

"Now just who is Baker Eastland and while you are informing us, exactly who are you?"

"My father is Manet Adams, the state congressman, and if you don't—"

Monk Mayfair rolled his eyes heavenward and took hold of his rusty pig-bristle hair. "This is startin' to give me one powerful headache."

Celia Adams fixed him with a withering blue-eyed stare, causing Ham Brooks to snicker. Monk and Ham were wonderful friends who enjoyed one another's misfortunes—particularly those they inflicted upon each other.

Growing more impatient with the congressman's spoiled daughter, Doc Savage demanded, "Baker Eastland—describe him, please."

The blonde gave a brief description of a brown-haired, brown-eyed man of average height and build. The description did not fit any of the four men who had been involved in the zany and elaborate fish business, Doc realized.

"Did Baker Eastland explain why he would want to meet with me?" Doc asked.

"No. Baker happens to be an important ichthyologist who worked for the government during the war,"

Celia Adams explained. "Now he's engaged in private research—not to mention being engaged to me. He's actually quite prominent in his field. I'm surprised you don't know of him. Perhaps you do not keep up with the latest advances in his field."

That remark brought sputters of mirth from Monk and Johnny. Ham tittered into his hand politely.

"Wait a minute," Doc said sharply. His face looked shocked. "You say your fiancé is an ichthyologist?"

A little taken aback by the bronze man's tone, Celia replied in a considerably calmer voice. "That's right," she said. "He studies sea life. Fish. Are you trying to tell me you don't know where he is?"

Doc ignored the question and described the four hoaxers he had lately encountered. "Know any of them?"

"No."

"Ever hear of a man named Max Wood?"

"Yes! He's a friend of Baker's. Or was. They were involved in a business arrangement together. It fell through. I don't know the details, but that was when Baker became scared or something, and decided he was going to see you. I was to come along, but he'd already left Quincy. I was too preoccupied with the wedding plans to pay much attention. . . ."

"Max Wood," Doc demanded. "Describe him."

"Well, he's sort of creepy, almost sinister," Celia Adams offered in a subdued voice, then belied her statement by describing a scholarly sounding individual of no overtly sinister attributes at all.

"You say this Wood is a sinister sort," Doc Savage pointed out, "but the man you describe possesses no unusual physical characteristics of any kind. Was there something in his background or actions that would lead you to label him so harshly?"

"Actually, I know very little about him," Celia Adams admitted defensively. "Only that he and Baker shared an interest in sea life, and they had been working on something together."

"But still you would characterize him as sinister?" Doc pressed.

Celia Adams looked out toward a long bank of windows through which the Hudson River was visible.

"You would have to know him to understand what I'm saying," she said vaguely. "I disliked Max Wood from the very first moment I laid eyes on him."

"A conundrum necessitating explanatory interlocution," Johnny Littlejohn remarked.

"There he goes again!" Celia said, throwing up her white-gloved hands like a fussy hen.

"What Johnny means," Ham interjected smoothly, "is Doc seems to know something we do not, and an explanation might clear some air." He neglected to add that Johnny's long words were his principal vice, which he mercilessly inflicted upon others for reasons known only to himself.

"All right," Doc Savage said. "Here's the gist of it." He ran through the last few hours' experiences, beginning with the first man-frightened-by-a-fish report to his eavesdropping on a strange plot directed at him. He included the futile chase to Long Island and the mysterious yellow seaplane, although it didn't exactly cover him in glory.

The others listened with expressions of mute puzzlement.

"Scared silver fish," Ham murmured when Doc was through talking. "Highly unlikely sources of terror."

"Sounds fishy to me, too," Monk put in for no other reason than that he knew it would elicit a pained wince from the proper Ham Brooks.

Celia Adams's comment was: "But that doesn't explain what happened to Baker. I demand that you find him at once! I demand it, do you hear?"

But Doc Savage had already moved across the library to a huge globe that was at least four feet in diameter.

"Where did you say you hailed from, Miss Adams?"

"Quincy. Quincy, Massachusetts. But what does that have to do with—"

"One of the men mentioned a place called Quincy," Doc remarked to no one in particular as he spun the globe. "There are several localities known as Quincy in the United States, but only one of which could be reached by flying in a generally northern direction from here. This one happens to be a city on the Massachusetts coast, just south of Boston."

Monk looked at the spot on the globe and predicted, "I guess we're going to Quincy."

Monk Mayfair had never heard of Quincy, Massachusetts, but that didn't stop him from reciting a travelogue of the city with facts that he gleaned from maps and an atlas he found in the plane, as they made their downleg approach to Quincy Bay.

"Quincy," Monk was saying, "is the only American city to produce two presidents, John Adams and John Quincy Adams. But the town is actually named after a Colonel John Quincy. The first iron blast furnace in the country was erected in Quincy. The first American railroad was built here in 1825. It wasn't for carrying passengers, though. They used it to shunt granite from Quincy Quarry across the Neponset River to Boston for the Bunker Hill Monument. It's a big shipbuilding town, too. Quincy Bay is separated from Boston Harbor by a headland called Squantum, named after the famous Indian, Squanto. It seems that it was on Squantum that Captain Miles Standish first met this Squanto. On the other hand, Squantum is Nargansett Indian lingo for 'angry god.' During Puritan days, a rascal named

Thomas Morton set up a trading post on a hill called Merry Mount at the other end of the beach, where he sold guns and liquor to the local redskins. He also erected a pagan maypole that upset Governor Bradford down in Plymouth Colony. He sent Miles Standish and some soldiers to Merry Mount to put a stop to Morton's wicked ways. They chopped down the maypole and hauled Morton away in chains."

Monk's tedious recitation, it was suspected, was offered for no better reason than to keep Celia Adams from getting a word in. Attractive as she was, no one seemed to enjoy her company. She sat alone, at the rear, fuming, which caused Johnny Littlejohn to remark to Doc Savage, "This is one outing Monk and Ham aren't fighting over a girl." The gaunt archælogist never used his long words on Doc.

The bronze man nodded as he ran through a cockpit check before landing. The flinty blonde hadn't exactly aroused his interest either, but then it was generally conceded that Doc was virtually woman-proof.

The plane was a twin-engine experimental jet. It had made the trip from New York in little less than an hour, so brief a time that Doc Savage hadn't bothered to pressurize the cabin.

"Hey!" Monk said in his immature voice. "According to this map, there's a naval air station in Squantum. We can land there."

Doc shook his head. "Too complicated. We'll set down in the water."

Monk evinced no surprise that Doc had decided on this unusual course. "This isn't exactly a village," he said, looking out the cockpit window at the fair-sized city stretching back from a long sandy line of beach where the water lapped placidly. "How are we going to find those four guys, assuming they're down there?"

Doc Savage didn't answer immediately, being absorbed in landing preparations. He dropped the wing flaps and dragged the bay. The water was placid. He brought the ship around again, changed the special aerfoil arrangement in the wings which made the landing run-out not much different from that of an ordinary propeller-driven craft, thereby allowing the ship to land where other jets could not. As on Quincy Bay.

The jet made its approach with a forward speed of less than sixty miles an hour. The water came up at them like a rippled blue sheet.

They hit with a jar, bounced; then the hull—designed for sea and snow landings—settled. Under low throttle, the bronze man goosed the jet toward shore, using the guide rudder to maneuver. It served as a water helm.

They anchored in a salt marsh at the north end of the beach, and waded through knee-high eelgrass to shore.

Celia Adams, with more than a trace of vinegar in her tone, repeated Monk's unanswered question:

"Just how *are* you going to find those men in a city this size? And we're wasting our time. Baker won't be here."

Doc Savage didn't respond to that; instead, he said: "I seem to recall a police station at the other end of the beach, and inland. We'll visit the local police for a start."

"But that's nearly a mile away!" Celia complained.

"More than a mile, in all," Doc replied. "We'd best get under way."

Celia Adams blinked her sharp blue eyes rapidly. Her mouth made preparatory shapes, but something in the bronze man's weird eyes quelled her feistiness.

They walked. The tide was out, and the sand consequently wet, where the early-winter cold hadn't frozen it in scabs of ice. A well-traveled road ran the length of the beach—Wollaston Beach, it was called, after a seaman known as Captain Wollaston, Monk informed them—and they trekked along the macadam sidewalk. At intervals, cars stood parked with their noses pointing oceanward, drivers enjoying sandwich lunches and the ocean view from the comfort of their vehicles.

Despite the inclement weather, the beach was not deserted. Several hardy individuals, their pants rolled up to the knees, ranged the patches of sand which the departing tide left behind, harvesting for clams with pails in one hand and clawed digging tools—clam forks—in the other.

Ham, noticing them, sniffed, "They don't seem to be having much luck. Their pails are empty."

"Too cold for clams," Monk said contrarily.

"Prevaricator," Johnny said of Monk, which caused Celia to regard the tall archæologist with disdain.

Monk didn't seem to mind being called a bald-faced liar by Johnny, which didn't mean he was unaware of Johnny's meaning. Monk never lost an opportunity to heckle or contradict Ham Brooks, and the lawyer invariably responded in kind. The two were good friends, but showed it in unusual ways.

They progressed a bare quarter mile, Ham anxiously glancing back at the moored jet, which had begun to attract the curious.

Celia Adams had kept a fuming silence like a slowly inflating balloon. It finally burst.

"How am I going to get married if you clowns don't find Baker! This is *ridiculous!* What are we doing here? Just because you overheard them mention Quincy, doesn't mean Baker came back here. And I don't even think that crazy fish business has anything to do with Baker's disappearance!" This tirade didn't appear directed at anyone in particular.

"I'm inclined to agree," Monk undertoned to Doc.

"The prospect of having a noise-maker like her for a breakfast partner doesn't exactly make me feel warm all over. I'll bet this Baker skipped out on her."

Doc said nothing, but his expression was a little weary. Women sometimes had that effect upon him.

The car was going a good seventy miles an hour when it came up from behind them, jumped the sidewalk, and smacked into the rocky seawall separating the sidewalk and beach. Before the men with the guns could leap out, Doc pushed Celia over and behind the seawall. He was not gentle about it. She went over like a flung rag doll and stayed down.

Monk next let out a spine-chilling whoop of pleasure and lunged for an opening car door. The driver had set one foot on the ground preparatory to emerging from behind the wheel. Then he saw Monk. He hastily withdrew the foot and tried to get the door shut. A big hairy paw plucked the door from his tugging hands. Then it pushed the wild-eyed driver into the gunman seated next to him. A shot punched a hole in the car roof. The gun clattered to the floorboards. Monk piled in.

Enthusiastically, the apish chemist began to re-upholster the front seat with its occupants.

Doc, Ham, and Johnny, not possessing Monk's primitive instincts, took a moment to assess the situation, during which two men stepped out of the back seat and pointed large weapons in their faces. The bores of the weapons had about the same empty expression as their eyes. They were two of the men from New York. One was the individual with carpet-tack eyes whom Doc recognized as the group's leader.

He said: "Let's have a show of hands."

Doc, Ham, and Johnny exchanged glances. Wordlessly, they raised their hands.

"O.K.," the straw boss said to his companion. "Now tranquilize King Kong there before he wrecks the car."

The second gunman stuck his head in the driver's window and, leaning in, chopped at something twice with the flat of his automatic. Monk's squawling subsided. After the pair in the front seat got themselves organized, Monk was tossed from the machine. Two battered men, one of them the sandy-haired man with sunburned ears who had feigned a fear of fish, alighted. The sunburned one promptly went rubber-kneed and fell on his face, unconscious.

At a nod from the straw boss, he was lugged out of sight.

"All right, now," the straw boss said with ferocious joy. "Let's grab off another car and cart these trouble-makers away from here." He looked around the damaged car. "Wait a minute! Wasn't there a girl with them a minute ago?"

The question was met by silence and stony regards.

"What about it, bronze guy?"

Doc Savage said nothing.

"O.K., have it your way," the leader said uneasily. "Two of you check around while I cover these birds."

They looked over the seawall—a logical first step—and found Celia Adams. She was huddled in the lee of the piled-stone seawall, playing possum.

"Jackpot," one said.

"Come on, you," the straw boss barked. "Get up."

When Celia refused to move, he snapped, "I said, get up!"

She jumped under the lash of his harsh words. Climbing to her feet, she said, "I'll have you know I'm Celia Adams, daughter of Congressman Manet Adams, and great-great granddaughter of Presidents John Adams and John Quincy Adams. My father is an important man in this town, and I—"

"Am a big noise all by yourself," the straw boss sneered. "We don't care much about you, your father, or any of your great and not-so-great grandfathers, so don't make us shoot you. I hate shooting famous people. It leads to all sorts of inconveniences."

Celia Adams meekly climbed over the seawall.

"What have you done with Baker?" she demanded through her obvious fright.

"We cut him up and fed him to the little fishes," the straw boss sneered.

Celia Adams put a white-gloved hand over her mouth and kept it there. Her face lost three shades of color.

"Good goin', Nate," a man guffawed. "That shut her up good."

The straw boss named Nate walked up to Doc Savage and showed his teeth in an unpleasant manner. "So you *did* know about this, after all."

Before Doc could reply, one of the men got another car going, having broken a window of a parked sedan in order to get at its ignition. "O.K.," he called back. "We're set now."

The prisoners were split up between the cars. Because one of the gunmen was unconscious, there was some fuss about arrangements. Finally, they decided to load their fallen member into the stolen car, along with Celia and the sleeping Monk, leaving two of them to ride with Doc, Ham, and Johnny.

They were pushing Celia into the back seat, their attention a little distracted, when Doc spoke quick words in Mayan, a language he used when he didn't wish to be understood by others outside his group, and simultaneously knocked the gun from the leader's hand.

Johnny Littlejohn fell upon the other gunman like

a set of hardwood sticks connected by elastic ropes. He seemed to tangle the man's limbs up in his own. A gun dropped to the ground, whereupon Johnny wordlessly and methodically pounded on the man's head with relentless, driving blows.

The third gunman shoved Celia into the back seat and brought out his gun. He waved it wildly, looking for a clear target, and settled on Ham Brooks, who was endeavoring to sneak up on him. The gun barked; Ham dived behind the seawall. The gunman rushed to the spot and collected himself a faceful of sand. His gun went off an inch from Ham's face, after which neither of them did any more fighting in deference to their angrily ringing eardrums.

The fight ended quickly.

Doc gathered the three functioning gunmen together.

"Suppose we have some answers," he suggested.

"Like what?" the leader retorted hotly.

"For instance, what is this about?"

The man looked aghast. "I thought you knew all about it!"

"Only what I overheard you saying outside my headquarters and what Miss Adams here has volunteered."

"Who the hell is she?"

"Baker Eastland's fiancée, if you must know. Now let's have it. All of it."

The captured attackers had been made to lean against the seawall, which being only about two feet high meant they were half-sitting, half-leaning against it. Nate, the man who seemed to be the straw boss of the quartet, looked queasy. He took his right wrist in his left hand and wet his lips nervously.

The gas pen must have been clipped to his sleeve because the cuff caught fire and immediately the air was full of choking, yellowish fumes.

"Tear gas!" Johnny yelled.

There was another brief melee, this time conducted under the most disorienting circumstances possible. Celia Adams let out a scream. Men collided. There were blows, but fortunately no guns went off.

Doc Savage was no less handicapped than the others. Lunging for a man, he barked both shins on the seawall and went down. From a sitting position, he reached out and upset such legs as he happened to encounter. He did this with his eyes pinched shut.

After a while, the noise and confusion subsided. Doc's leaking eyes cleared. He found, in succession, Johnny, Monk—still out cold—and Ham Brooks.

The four gunmen and Celia Adams were gone. At first the bronze man couldn't understand how that could be, because both cars were still present; then he remembered that there had been several small boats anchored not far off shore.

Sure enough, a small shell of a motorboat sputtered out into the bay. He could see Celia Adams in the boat, along with three of the men. The legs of the fourth one—the one still unconscious—dangled off the port side.

Ham Brooks made a disgusted noise in his throat, then fetched some bone-chilling seawater in his hat to pour over Monk Mayfair's face. Ham poured it slowly, pausing often in fierce enjoyment. The fact that the brine was having no effect seemed not to discourage the lawyer in the slightest.

Johnny turned to Doc Savage. "Reckon we can get to the plane in time to follow them from the air?"

The reply never came because the police arrived next.

The police came in a black and white prowl car. They emerged wearing almost identical unhappy expressions. First they surveyed the two damaged vehicles and then they demanded an explanation.

"Let's hear about this, starting with who the hell you all are," the taller of the pair said.

"I'm Clark Savage, Jr.," Doc Savage said, which took the orneriness out of both of the cops. They turned sweet and polite and solicitous. They had heard of Doc Savage, they said. Could they be of assistance? they wanted to know. Were they—meaning Doc and his party—in Quincy to look into the fish mystery?

"What fish mystery?" Doc asked sharply. One of the cops jumped in startlement.

"Why, it's the damndest thing," the shorter one offered. "For the past two weeks, there hasn't been any fish in Quincy Bay. And this is an excellent fishing spot. Even the clam diggers are coming away empty-handed."

III

THE ICHTHYOLOGIST

Doc Savage's state and federal credentials had the entire Quincy police force falling over the bronze man and his aides. They were at the city police station, a three-story sandstone edifice overlooking a well-manicured cemetery. Doc was using a telephone in the office of the captain of police, whose name was Slattery.

Doc had already made half a dozen calls. The Coast Guard had reported the progress of the fleeing motorboat as far as the Boston airport. From there, the four men and Celia Adams had taken a light plane—the NC numbers were the same as the seaplane Doc had seen take off from Long Island. Doc had requested that the plane not be hindered in any way, but every flying field in New England was alerted to watch out for it.

While awaiting word, Doc Savage was asked by the captain of police if there was anything he desired. "Any little thing at all," as the captain phrased it.

"Has my associate Monk awoken yet?" Doc asked.

"Mr. Brooks is working him over with smelling salts."

Just then, the results of Ham Brooks's ministrations charged into the captain's office, pursuing Ham Brooks himself.

Ham bowled past Captain Slattery, looked about frantically for another door, and, seeing none, set his

30

back to a heavy maple coatrack and unsheathed his sword cane at the bellowing form of Monk Mayfair.

"Stay back, you simian mistake of nature!" Ham warned.

Monk waved an open bottle of smelling salts. "Not until I give you a taste of your own medicine," Monk roared.

"Monk," Doc warned.

"I mean it this time," Monk snarled. "I've had it with this ambulatory pork chop. I woke up not five minutes ago with this bottle of smelling salts practically shoved up one nostril. That was bad enough, but when I saw that I was in a jail cell, I naturally wanted to know why."

"Under the circumstances, it was the most logical place to put an unconscious man," Doc explained.

"I know that now," Monk growled, eyeing Ham, "but this shyster spun me a story that I had accidentally killed a man back at the beach and I had come down with amnesia. He told me I was on death row and he had come to say good-bye, since I was scheduled for the hot seat at midnight. I was never so scared in my life."

"Not true," Ham taunted. "The first time you ever looked into a mirror should take that prize."

Monk roared, lifting his long furry arms. Ham feinted with his cane. A sticky chemical daubed on the tip gleamed. It was an anæsthetic compound, and only that, not the threat of the blade itself, kept the hairy chemist at bay.

"Monk," Doc said levelly, "I'd like you to return to the plane and use your equipment to collect water samples from Quincy Bay." Doc turned to Captain Slattery. "Would you mind having one of your officers give my aide a ride back?"

"Not at all, Mr. Savage," the police captain said, eyeing the two would-be combatants with concern.

Then, to everyone's surprise, Monk immediately

lowered his arms and Ham Brooks unconcernedly returned his sword to its ebony sheath.

"Anyplace special you want me to take the sample from?" Monk asked Doc Savage in a suddenly amiable voice.

"Take one from either end of the beach," the bronze man instructed. "Then go out into the middle of the bay and collect a third. Not too far out."

"Gotcha, Doc. Catch you later, shyster," Monk called to Ham Brooks. He left the room without a word.

Less than an hour passed before Doc received a call from a private field on the north shore of Massachusetts, informing him that the plane had just landed there. Doc thanked the field manager and hung up.

Monk strolled in at that point, carrying an equipment case under one long arm. He gave it a hearty spank. "I did like you asked, Doc."

"Notice anything unusual?" Doc Savage asked.

"I noticed there wasn't any fish in the water."

"We knew that."

"One of them clam diggers fed me a nice yarn," Monk added. "He related as how one night about two weeks back, the entire bay up and turned black."

"Black?"

"That's what he said, black."

Doc turned to Captain Slattery. "Know anything about this?"

Captain Slattery looked uncomfortable. "There was some wild talk around that time, yeah, but by the time we heard the reports, it was morning, and the bay was as blue as lake water. We figured the reports were mistaken. There was no moon that night. If the bay had turned black under those conditions, how would anyone be able to tell?"

"The people who reported this," Doc inquired, "they were local citizens?"

"Yeah," Slattery admitted. "Why?"

"Presumably, locals would know the normal appearance of the water on a moonless night. They would not normally have made such a mistake."

The captain rubbed his jaw thoughtfully. "I hadn't thought of that," he said slowly.

"We'll be going now, captain," Doc said.

The police drove them back to their jet and all but tried to push Doc's craft into the air by hand.

The hull pontoon carved a long wake out over the bay, got on step, and vaulted into the sky. The sky was the same color as the bay. Blue. But it was darkening with the approach of night.

"Funny thing about those vanished fish," Johnny was saying after they began climbing to the north. "I wonder if it ties in with this mystery we're investigating?"

"I don't see how," Ham snorted. "Besides, just because the fish disappear from one bay doesn't seem to add up to all that much in my book."

"Much as I hate to admit it," Monk added, "this shyster is right. Those cops said the missing-fish business was limited to Quincy Bay, so it doesn't amount to anything threatening. Besides, don't fish migrate, just like birds? Maybe the fish in Quincy Bay are just in a migrating mood. So what's the big deal?"

"Ever see a fish bowl that wasn't taken care of properly?" Johnny asked, blowing a dust speck off his monocle, which hung from his lapel by a ribbon. It was not actually an eyepiece, but a magnifying glass carried that way for convenience.

"Yeah. What's that got to do with it?"

"When you don't keep a fish tank clean," Johnny began in a lecturelike tone, "the water gets scummy with algae. That's why catfish are often put in home tanks: they help scour them clean by their scavenging habits. Take the catfish away, stop feeding the fish, and the food chain breaks down. Everything dies. It works the same way, on a larger scale, in the ocean. Remove the plants, for instance, and there will be no oxygen for fish to breathe. Conversely, if you take away the fish, the plants will die off, because the fish exhale carbon dioxide, which sea plants need to survive. Even if you were to remove only one or two species of fish, you would destroy the food chain because some fish are food for others, and some, by eating still other fish, serve to keep those fish populations down. And then there is the matter of human dependence upon fish. There is a big fishing industry in this country. Suppose all the fish were to depart from, say, the East Coast. It would result in economic catastrophe."

Monk and Ham digested that for some minutes. Finally, Monk said: "Aw, you're just building a castle of words—even if they are small words for a change."

Doc Savage did not take part in the conversation. He was more than a little chagrined with his performance back in Quincy. He had counted upon the sight of his experimental jet aircraft drawing his quarry out in the open, should they be present. The ruse had worked, yet the attacker had managed to catch Doc and his party off-guard. He was intensely disgusted about that development. At length, he decided what had gone wrong. He hadn't alerted his men to the plan, and the reason was that each time he had been about to, Celia Adams had demanded an explanation for his actions, and this had caused him to perversely hold back.

Doc decided that he didn't like Celia Adams.

The air field was small and situated near a wooden bridge that connected the coastal town of Newburyport with what area maps called Plum Island. From the air, Plum Island resembled an elongated amoeba of sand perhaps a mile in length and separated from land by a small expanse of tidal flat and salt marsh. Like an oversized barber pole, a small red and white lighthouse thrust up from the north end of the island, which Monk Mayfair informed them was named for the plentiful wild plums that grew on it. Monk had his head buried in the atlas again. Ham Brooks was the target of his recitation this time.

It was Johnny Littlejohn who brought the beached whales to their attention.

"Doc," he said. "I believe those are blackfish."

"I see them," the bronze man said. "And you are right. Those *are* blackfish."

"Where?" Monk Mayfair said, looking out to see with an eager face.

"Not in the water, you gossoon," Ham snorted. "They're up on the beach."

Monk's twinkling eyes raked the sandy side of the island. They went wide at the sight of the blubbery black shapes that sat in the shadow of the lighthouse like a row of sardines fallen out of a tin.

"For God's sake!" Monk exploded. "There's seven of them!" The hairy chemist turned to Doc. "Think it has anything to do with this fish hocus-pocus?"

"It is another thing to investigate," Doc told him, scanning the beach. On the island's long eastern side, waves crashed and spent themselves against long jetties of seaweed-festooned granite blocks.

"No way to land among those breakers," Monk judged.

Doc nodded, as he requested clearance from the field.

It was a dirt field intended for private craft. A line of gaudy one- and two-engine planes were staked down along one side of the field, like expectant birds of prey. It would be a difficult landing.

Doc took the wind direction and speed from the operations manager and brought the jet around into the wind. It was blowing twenty miles an hour, which would help decrease airspeed. Doc adjusted the aerfoil curvature until airspeed had dropped below one hundred and fifty and he lowered the wheels, noting the gear locking lights as they turned green.

The high-pressure dual tires hit, and stayed in contact with the ground as the jet's flaps dug into the wind. The end of the field came up on them swiftly. Doc eased the wheel brakes into play.

With a decreasing whine coming from both engines, the jet lurched to a stop. Doc shut down No. 1 and turned his attention to No. 2. The turbine blades wound down to silence.

Monk was the first one out of the jet. Doc climbed down last.

A roly-poly man came running out of the operations shack—shack was about the size of it—with a lot of questions about Doc's jet. The bronze man cut him off impatiently, and asked some questions of his own.

"Sure," he was told by the shivering operations manager. "The ship you describe landed about an hour or so ago. The pilot asked the way to the *Gremlin*, then he and the others headed for the island on foot."

"*Gremlin?*"

"One of the cottages on the island. They all have names, kinda like boats. The *Gremlin* is owned by Max Wood; I tried to tell them Max only spends his summers here, but they didn't seem to care about that."

"Ever hear of a Baker Eastland?" Ham put in, dark eyes snapping.

"Sure. Old Baker's a swell egg. Friend of Max's— and mine. But Baker ain't here either. I'd know about it if he was. Besides, it's off-season. Only die-hards on the island right now. And a few island sightseers come to see the whales."

"How many in the party?" Doc asked.

"Four. Five counting the girl." The operations manager gave concise, accurate descriptions of the four gunmen and Celia Adams. None resembled the Max Wood of Celia Adams's description.

"When did the whales beach?" Doc asked at last.

"Yesterday. But we've had a rash of beachings for weeks now. Never seen anything like it in all my years on the island."

They borrowed a car and drove it over the bridge, past the salt marsh and onto the island. The stink of exposed tidal flat assailed their nostrils. On either side of the road, cones of salt hay lay piled on wood staddles.

The *Gremlin* was easy to find, there being only one road worthy of the term. Past the church and on the right. It was a rude clapboard box of a weather-beaten thing sitting on the sand, close enough to the water to be in peril during storms, and the color of yellow cream with a gray tinge in it.

Doc drove past it. There was no sign of habitation, and they hadn't passed any of the quartet of gunmen or Celia Adams walking on foot—not that they really expected to at this late hour—but the absence of life hanging about the seemingly uninhabited *Gremlin* stimulated Doc's sense of caution.

"We gonna double back and sneak up on it?" Monk wondered.

"The whales first," Doc said.

The road—it was of gravel, not blacktop—petered out in the vicinity of the squat peppermint stick of a lighthouse. Doc pulled over to the side. They got out and trudged toward the Nubian shapes of the stranded whales.

As they approached, they heard the forlorn blowing

sounds the whales made. One would blow, then another, and on down the line to the last. They were like a sad wind section.

Doc Savage eased his way into the crowd. It consisted of mostly locals hugging themselves against the chill sea wind and the helplessness of Man before an unexplainable force of Nature.

"Jove, Doc," Ham Brooks breathed, examining the monsters from a cautious distance, "what kind of power could shove seven live whales clear up on dry sand like this?"

Instead of replying, the bronze man circled the whales, his flake-gold eyes animated.

Johnny Littlejohn answered for Doc. "Whale beachings are not uncommon," he told the others. "But no one has yet been able to explain why perfectly healthy creatures such as these strand themselves in this manner, for death is the inevitable result."

"You mean," Monk squeaked, "these whales are committing suicide!"

"Actually, they are blackfish, a species of small whale. They are commercially valuable, because their heads contain an oil which can be used as a lubricant for certain delicate mechanisms. The oil is found in a cranial organ known as the melon. And, yes, suicide is one of the hypotheses most frequently expounded to explain the phenomenon of spontaneous whale strandings."

"They do look kinda sad-eyed, at that," Monk admitted.

"If you ask me," Ham joined in, "these beasts look positively scared."

"Nobody asked you, shyster," Monk said unkindly.

Doc Savage drifted back and leveled an arm in the direction of the water. Night was falling, but frequent splashings could be seen on the ocean's surface.

"Have you noticed how active the water is?" Doc asked.

"Great grief!" Ham exclaimed. "Are more coming?"

"No," the bronze man said quietly. "Those are ordinary game fish." He listened to the splashings a moment, then remarked: "I think it is time to investigate the *Gremlin*."

They returned to the car.

A quarter mile short of the cottage, they pulled into a sandy driveway between two tumbledown duplex cottages and started off on foot.

"Say, Doc," Monk asked as they worked their way along the beach. His big feet made the sand under them complain endlessly. It was now night. Above, hanging poised in the sea wind like bleached bats, sea gulls scolded them with raucous voices. Waves gnashed at the breakers with monotonous regularity, throwing up foam and cold spray, and crawling back in sullen retreat. "Why do you suppose they all lit out for this sand dune?"

"Because that Baker Eastland is probably holed up here," Ham put in snidely.

"Yeah, but how'd they pounce on that fact—if true—so sudden?"

"I'll bet that Celia spilled those particular beans," offered Johnny, whose general opinion of women was not generous.

"Then why didn't she breathe a word to us?" Monk demanded.

"If you recollect, Celia Adams is nothing if not a contrary morsel," Johnny pronounced flatly.

That sounded about correct to Doc Savage, but he kept his thoughts within himself.

Cottages were sprinkled on either side of the main road, so they slipped in between these in order to approach the *Gremlin*.

It was well that they did so because it enabled them to spot five shadowy figures attempting to do the same from the cottage's opposite side. Their skulking attitude as they moved into the lee of a ramshackle structure marked them as suspicious. The automatics in their hands were discernible by their familiar square shapes.

One of their number struggled with another. A hand lashed out, producing a sharp slap of a sound. The struggling figure settled down. Its crouching outline was unmistakably feminine.

"We know who *they* are," Ham breathed.

"Let's see if we can beat their time," Monk said fiercely, and his homely features took on a rock-cracking expression.

"Good idea," Doc stated. They set off at a dead run across the sand and got to the cottage's screen-enclosed veranda, where they crouched low.

"A manifestation of crepuscular invisibility," Johnny ventured, meaning that the dark had kept them from being seen.

Doc hit the door, and the others followed him in.

"Eastland!" Doc Savage hissed. "This is Doc Savage."

The noise of their own breathing as they hugged a dusty, threadbare rug was the only sound. It wasn't reassuring. The room was dark, but cracks of pale, seeping light outlined a door.

Doc crawled to this, acutely aware that if the missing ichthyologist was here, he was probably armed and frightened enough to fall back upon wild shooting in a crunch.

"Eastland!" Doc rapped out. "Your enemies are on our heels. They have Miss Adams with them. You'd better come to some swift decisions before we're all prisoners, or worse."

That did it. A brown-haired, brown-eyed young

man stepped through the open door. He had a revolver, but if his careless handling was any guide, not much familiarity with its use. His face wore a tan that looked dusty because apprehension had drained the skin beneath it of blood.

"I know about them," he rasped. "They've been out there for over an hour, just skulking around. They're waiting for something." Baker Eastland—he fit the description Celia Adams had given in New York—looked haggard. "You *are* Doc Savage," he said after they had found their feet. "How on earth did you find me?"

Doc sketched in the details, beginning with the bizarre fish hijinks back in New York, finishing with, "That is just the tip of the iceberg, as far as we are aware. We don't know any more about this mystery."

Baker Eastland cast a wary eye out a window. "They're still out there." Doc went to his side. "Maybe if I tried to pick them off," Eastland suggested hopefully, "we could round off the odds in our favor."

Frowning, Doc took away his gun. "You ever fire one of these before?"

Eastland looked contrite. "No."

"Ever kill a man?"

"Of course not!" he exploded.

"Then this is no time to start." Doc broke open the pistol and extracted the shells. He placed the weapon on a table, from which Monk Mayfair surreptitiously retrieved it, along with the shells. Monk gave the appearance of an amiable vulgarian, but his nature included a strong streak of blood-thirstiness. He hid the reloaded revolver under his coat.

A car drew to a halt on the road while they were assessing their position. Both Doc and Eastland moved to another room to get a better view, while the others kept watch over the skulking gunmen, who hadn't moved much from their places of concealment. The room was bare except for countless fish mounted on polished wooden trophy plaques. They seemed to hug the shadows, holding their collective breaths against some impending menace.

It was pitch-black now, and there was no moon to illuminate the situation. Several men stepped from the car, and one of them uncorked a long, high-pitched whistle. The signal was answered in kind.

"Hey!" Monk yelled suddenly. "These guys are moving!"

Doc raced back in alarm, only to discover that the gunmen had merely broke and run for the lately arrived vehicle. He rejoined Baker Eastland—Monk, Ham, and Johnny in tow.

"Max Wood is here!" Eastland moaned, as if speaking of Old Nick himself. "I recognize his profile."

"Wood is behind this fish mystery?" Doc queried.

"Yes. He . . . he was my friend. Or I had considered him such before all this hell broke loose."

"How about letting us see more of this iceberg," Doc suggested.

Eastland cast a pained look out at the car and its huddled figures. "Max Wood is a scientist, a marine biologist. At least he told me he was. Later, I had reason to doubt his claim, although he was very learned. I developed something during the war—I used to work for the Navy's Woods Hole Oceanographic Institute— but didn't complete my work until the shooting had ended. It was just as well. I had discovered a horrible thing. But Wood wanted it. I met him six months ago and . . ." Eastland's voice trailed off. He swallowed. "I'm ashamed to say that I sold him the secret. After I had time to think about it, I realized that Wood intended no good, and I tried to buy it back, but he was adamant. We had a terrible fight. He tried to kill me, but I got away."

"Was that when you tried to reach me?"

"Yes, that's right. I once attended a lecture you'd given on the diversity of scalation among extinct *osteostracans* and *anaspids* of the *Cephalaspidomorphi* class, and of course I'd heard of your career of righting wrongs and punishing—"

"And what happened next?" Doc prompted.

Eastland withdrew from the window harriedly. He faced Doc Savage, wearing a tight expression. Despite his relative youth, his features were as element-seamed as an old salt's. "I was nearly ambushed on the way to New York," he said. "I realized I was being followed. They found out I was bound for your headquarters. So I doubled back to Massachusetts. I thought I was doing a clever thing by hiding in Wood's own summer cottage. We spent some time here last summer before all this happened. I don't understand how they could have guessed where I'd be."

"We have a theory about that," Doc told him.

"What's that?"

Instead of answering, Doc asked a question: "Had you mentioned this cottage as a hiding place to your fiancée?"

"I believe I did. I told her that if things got tough, I could wait out the winter up here. But Celia would never betray me like that. She's a very closemouthed girl."

Monk snorted. "From what we seen of her, she's a fountain of comment. In fact, if we ever get her back, you could do us a big favor and show us where her comment cut-off switch is."

Baker Eastland had no response to that. New worry settled over his tanned features.

"Doc!" Ham hissed warningly. "They're moving in on us!"

It was true. Fully nine darkened figures had fanned

out and were approaching the *Gremlin* cautiously. Doc spotted one submachine gun and knew that the thin walls of the cottage would be absolutely no protection against the high-caliber slugs.

The bronze man stripped off his coat, wrapped it around his hard metallic fist, and popped some glass from the window.

"Wood!" he called. "Don't try it! We have gas." It was true. They all carried capsules of anæsthetic gas, but under the circumstances they had little hope of felling all of the attackers before bullets flew.

There was no answer. Doc plucked a capsule from his coat, and let fly at the submachine gunner. That one advanced two paces and dug his face into the sand. He didn't move after that.

"One down," Ham whispered.

The attackers changed tactics then. Three of them withdrew to the car, where Celia Adams was being held by the shadowy figure Baker had identified as Max Wood. They held their weapons ready while the others came on.

"This isn't good," Doc rapped. "They intend to make us exhaust our gas supply. They evidently know it renders itself ineffective within forty seconds of release." Doc's hypnotic flake-gold eyes whirled more rapidly.

"Wood!" he called urgently.

The shadowy figure stood silent, as if mocking their impotence. Doc could not make the figure out except as a lean, black form, like a scarecrow at midnight. Wood's stocky aloofness imparted itself to the bronze man as a manifestation of the embodiment of cold evil. He was startled to find himself shaking off a momentary chill that had nothing to do with the cold.

The man gestured sharply and withdrew to the shelter of the waiting vehicle.

"They're going to massacre us!" Baker Eastland wailed, and the others knew that this was very likely.

* * *

The wall flew to pieces then.

Bullets tore through the thin clapboard like angry bees. The wall was all seasoned wood, but for the window Doc had already broken, so there were no treacherous shards of glass, only jacketed lead and flying splinters. A submachine gun stitched back and forth, back and forth, while pistols snapped and chewed bristly holes.

They dropped to the floor. No one escaped the storm of lead. Monk, unluckily, caught two bullets full in the chest and hopped and flew back into another room, like a comical frog. He bellowed once, but that was all. Ham huddled in a corner, arms shielding his head, his ever-present sword cane still clutched in his hands. A bullet popped a hole in the back of his coat. He coughed once.

Other holes appeared in the clothes of Doc Savage and Johnny Littlejohn. Johnny shifted position on the floor after the first bone-jarring impact, then lay still. Stoically, Doc endured the assault on his person. His giant form seemed to absorb each impact like a human sponge.

Then the bullets stopped.

Baker Eastland, his left arm stringing yarns of blood, looked about. "Oh my God, they're all dead!" Fright took him, then—sheer, headlong, maddening panic. He dashed for the door, covered twenty yards, and tried to bury himself in a sand dune. His legs stuck out, however, and he was pulled free by two men.

"Well, well, looky here," one crowed. "We found us an ostrich, didn't we?"

"Whaddya got to say for yourself, ostrich?"

"Dead . . ." Eastland moaned. "They're all dead. . . ."

"Hear that, Nate? He says Doc Savage and the others are dead."

The one called Nate—the group's apparent straw

boss—cradled a rifle and indicated the *Gremlin* with his jaw. "We'd better check it out to be sure."

But the scream of sirens put a damper on that notion. A whistle signal sounded in the night again, and they dragged the wounded ichthyologist to the waiting car. The car, fortunately for them, was a big, roomy model equipped with old-fashioned running boards. Such individuals as who could not fit inside clung to this. They bestowed ragged fire upon the police car as they passed it going in the opposite direction, away from the island.

The police were a little short-tempered with Doc Savage, inasmuch as they had just been sniped at and the bronze man was not inclined to answer questions when he felt pursuit to be of paramount importance. The police were not going anywhere, they told him, because their car was all shot up, and they'd be damned twice over if they were going to let anyone else do their chasing for them, federal commissions or not.

The stalemate persisted in the face of Doc's insistence that there had been a kidnaping and several attempted murders. Hot words flew, but the cops were not budging.

"So give, big guy," one of the cops demanded.

Finally, Doc answered the bulk of their questions, took their badge numbers, and promised dire things if he and his associates were not allowed to continue their investigation.

The cops caved in. The bronze man could be very persuasive. But in deference to their pride, they asked one last question.

"Savage, you say these gunmen opened fire on that cottage yonder while you were in it and escaped with this itthy... itthy... fish expert?"

"That is substantially correct," Doc said, neglecting

to mention the anaesthetized gunman whose sleeping form Monk Mayfair had industriously covered with sand before the police arrived.

"I'd like to know, then, how you four gents managed to avoid dying after acquiring tiny little holes all over your bodies."

"Bullet-proof undergarments," Doc replied brittlely, an answer which so dumbfounded the two cops that they took their leave there and then. On foot.

Johnny walked up to the bronze man with an odd look on his scholarly visage.

"I played a hunch and asked around that crowd yonder," he said. "You know what they told me?"

Doc Savage looked his question.

"The fishing's fine up here. In fact, it's been remarkable since last month. Some of the locals are even claiming they're catching deep-water cod just off shore."

"Blazes!" That was from Monk. They joined him.

Monk and Ham had unearthed the unconscious gunman, who had fallen facedown in the sand. Monk lifted up the man's face by his hair. It was encrusted with sand. The homely chemist slapped it loose with lip-smacking enthusiasm.

The revealed face was wide, with a sloping forehead and an underslung jaw that gave it a toadlike aspect. Mouth hanging open, the man breathed noisily through his caked nostrils. But it was his narrow, pinched-shut eyes that caught and held their attention.

Monk's mouth was working in astonishment, so Ham had to say it:

"This person is a *Japanese!*"

IV

PACIFIC TRAIL

Upon reviving, the toad-faced Japanese explained that his name was W. J. Tsumi, and he was "So sorry. English not very good. Excuse, please."

That was the extent of his conversation on the trip from Plum Island back to Doc's New York headquarters. They hadn't pressed him, being preoccupied with tracing the plane which had taken off from the Newburyport air field with Baker Eastland and Celia Adams. Actually, two planes had taken off, they learned from the operations manager, Max Wood having arrived in a second craft not long after Doc had touched down. A second alert of New England airports had garnered no results whatsoever, so Doc elected to return to New York with their prisoner after taking samples from the waters where the blackfish had beached.

The Japanese, in addition to having been named W. J. Tsumi, was short, brown, clean-shaven and adept in Bushido Judo techniques, as Monk Mayfair found after giving the prisoner an extra-hard push into their reception room. He discovered himself hanging over both sides of the massive inlaid table very suddenly.

"The last guy who did that was triplets," Monk growled, advancing on the Jap.

Monk tried to sweep the Japanese up in a bear

hug. The little fellow eluded the hairy chemist's thick arms and took hold of one thick wrist. This time, Monk crashed into the ancient office safe.

Ham Brooks pulled his cane apart and pricked the Japanese on the arm with the half of the stick that was a sword cane. The chemical tip put him to sleep promptly, thereby cheating Monk out of his revenge.

Doc Savage gathered up the unconscious Japanese man and carried him into the adjoining laboratory, where he went to work preparing a syringe for charging.

He injected the man in the forearm, swabbed the puncture with a bit of cotton dipped in alcohol, and then directed his attention to Monk's equipment case.

"Anything I can do to help?" Monk asked as Doc removed four stoppered tubes of somewhat cloudy seawater. Three of these were the water samples from Quincy Bay. The fourth was a sample taken from Plum Island. Doc set the latter off to one side.

"Stay handy," Doc said, as he racked the remaining three tubes on a long work table and collected test equipment from glass-fronted cases. "Johnny, you have some knowledge of ocean denizens. See if you can identify the likeness our friends painted in front of our headquarters. It may be important."

"A pleasure," Johnny said.

As Johnny left the laboratory, Monk pulled up a stool to watch Doc Savage at work. Although himself one of the world's leading industrial chemists, Monk Mayfair enjoyed watching the bronze man operate. Ham excused himself. It was presumed that the foul-smelling chemicals Doc had opened had something to do with this decision.

Doc worked in silence. He poured water from each sample into shallow dishes. These he placed over a trio of Bunsen burners which fed off a single gas line. He heated the dishes slowly.

Monk lost track of Doc's tests, so rapidly did the bronze man work. He analyzed the heated samples under the microscope, occasionally turning his head to check on the state of their prisoner.

He was engrossed in his analysis when Johnny Littlejohn returned, balancing a thick reference book in one hand.

Doc looked up.

"*Sphoeroides nephelus*, order *tetraodontiformes*, family *tetraodontidae*," Johnny announced in his precise, scholarly voice.

Doc nodded as if the words confirmed his own suspicions. He returned to his labors.

"What's that mean?" Monk wanted to know.

"Puffer fish," Johnny told him, clapping the book shut. He withdrew.

A half hour later, the Japanese was mumbling in an overstuffed chair like a drunken man. His words were a slurry brand of Japanese, which was no barrier to Doc and Johnny, both of whom were fluent in that particular language. They had gathered around him as soon as he had begun speaking.

"What's he sayin', Doc?" Monk demanded for the third time.

Doc's steady questioning had elicited what to Monk sounded like rambling nonsense. Doc confirmed this supposition.

"Truth serum is hardly reliable stuff," Doc said unhappily. "Even the type we use is not much different from that employed by the federal authorities, in that it merely lowers the resistance of a subject sufficiently to diminish the ability to concentrate. Lacking full possession of his faculties, like a drunk, his subconscious mind will rise to the surface and he will speak unguardedly when questioned properly. But the truth serum will not, strictly speaking, extract the truth."

"Are you tryin' to tell us all he's spoutin' is banana oil?" Monk demanded.

"I wish I knew. He appears preoccupied with some vague and fantastic plot against his home nation, Japan. I can't get any specifics out of him except for an address in Tokyo. It may or may not be important."

"Did you notice how he repeats one word over and over?" Johnny asked.

"I did," Doc said.

"How anyone can tell one word from another in that gobble of sounds is beyond me," Monk offered.

"It sounded like *fugu*," Johnny pointed out. "Coincidence?"

"Doubtful," Doc Savage said, grim-toned.

"What's a *fugu*?" Monk demanded.

"A puffer fish," Doc told him.

Monk scratched his bristled nubbin of a head. "This business sure has its whacky side."

Ham Brooks entered from the library.

Doc looked up from studying the prisoner's slack, toadlike visage. "Anything?" he asked.

"Darn it, yes. I've been busier than a one-armed juggler spreading the alert for those planes. A field in Millard, Missouri, reported that both planes landed and refueled over an hour ago, then headed west. That was before they got the word there, of course. They have enough high-test aviation gas to make the coast."

Doc ordered his men to man the phones, while he returned to his study of the seawater samples. He put each sample through a battery of tests, none of which were conclusive. He was about to turn his attention to the Plum Island sample, which he had as yet not touched, when Ham Brooks interrupted. Monk and Johnny were with him.

"The plane reached California a few minutes ago," Ham reported.

"Where did it land?" Doc inquired.

"It didn't. It flew straight out to sea."

"Well, one thing's for sure," Monk announced, casting a villainous glance at their all-but-unconscious captive, "they're sure not heading for Japan."

"Don't be too certain of that," Doc said, reaching for the untested seawater sample. "Because we are."

The canal pilot officially took charge of the submarine at the Gatun Locks. Doc Savage didn't like the idea, but he had no choice in the matter. That was the way they ran the Panama Canal. The pilot boarded. They exchanged some polite words, and the pilot directed that they enter the first lock.

The submarine, its Diesel motors shut off, passed through the massive double steel doors that were the Canal's Caribbean entrance and into the concrete enclosure. The dual doors valved closed and additional water invaded the lock, rapidly raising the water level until the submarine had been lifted high enough to venture into the second lock, which sat at a higher elevation.

A warning bell started jangling. The inland doors groaned open.

They passed into the second lock and the process was repeated. The third and last lock was level with Gatun Lake. When they passed out of that one, the little electric locomotives called mules—which ran on undulating railroad tracks on either side of the locks and towed the sub along—released their cables.

The pilot left them, and the *Helldiver* got under way on its own power. After riding the ingenious system of water elevators, they had come to the Canal proper.

Monk and Johnny climbed out on the sub's razor

spine for fresh air. After a day and a half, they had had their fill of the sub's greasy interior.

The sun was high and the day balmy. The violet flowers and green stems of water hyacinths floated past them. They were steaming along a section of the Canal between locks. Here, tropical jungle and vicious sawgrass grew along each bank. They might have been navigating a natural river instead of a manmade feat of engineering.

"Aren't them trees over yonder?" Monk asked Johnny, referring to what seemed to be huge water plants.

"They never bothered to uproot the forest when they flooded this valley," Johnny said. He was using small words again. It was suspected that he'd run out of the jawbreaker variety in the course of the trip. "We'll have to watch the screws. They could get tangled by water growth."

"Beats me why Doc pulled this old scow out of mothballs," Monk mumbled, regarding the grease stains on his shirt tiredly.

"Doc always has his reasons," Johnny reminded.

Monk was referring to the *Helldiver*. The submarine had been built back in the days of the polar pioneers for an under-the-Arctic expedition by an explorer, now deceased. The sub had, in fact, made one such trip, but that was long ago and it was now an ungainly-looking antique, with its sledlike hull runners and collapsible conning tower. The bronze man had acquired the *Helldiver* in the course of that adventure and she had seen them through some bloody trials before Doc had more or less retired her to experimental status, taking her out of dry dock only to test some new submarine invention of his own devising.

"Flying would have been faster," Monk continued. "I know we couldn't take the jet because of fuel restrictions, but we coulda used a long-range bus for the hop."

"Doc has his reasons," Johnny repeated. "I'll bet it has something to do with this fish business."

"That's another thing! What're we doing heading for Japan all of a sudden? One minute we're listening to that little guy babble about Tokyo and puffer fish, next Doc is hustling us and him out to sea. Seems like a powerful lot of traveling without sound reasoning behind it."

"Doc must think that Max Wood has bundled himself and his prisoners off to the Land of the Rising Sun—if any of the latter are still alive, which I wonder about."

Monk snorted. "That Celia Adams has probably got those guys all talked half to death by now. That girl's my idea of a tall glass of nothing at all."

"I'm more worried about this fish business," Johnny said, polishing his monocle. "What caused them to vanish from Quincy Bay? And where did they go?"

"Are you back to that?" Monk growled in exasperation.

Ham joined them topside to add a third corner to the impending row.

The planes—there were three of them—waited until the *Helldiver* had entered the narrow Gaillard Cut channel at the eastern end of the Isthmus of Panama before attacking.

They danced down out of the sun and, taking turns, began strafing the submarine with their wing-mounted 7.7-caliber machine guns.

Monk, Ham, and Johnny, hearing the chopping sounds of bullets striking formerly peaceful water, dropped overboard and clung to the hull runners while the planes chewed futilely at the submarine's hull. After all three had passed, they wasted no time getting below and dogging the deck hatch.

Doc Savage met them.

"What's happening?" he demanded. "That sounded like an air attack!"

"It is," Ham said wildly. "Three planes, military type. They looked like Japanese Zeros, but without markings. They just up and pounced on us!"

"What would Zeros be doing in the Canal?" Doc asked, plunging forward. "The Japanese military apparatus was dismantled years ago."

Doc took the controls, spun wheels and threw levers.

The *Helldiver* sank hastily as the planes executed their second pass, this time coughing down twenty-millimeter cannon shells. Switching to electric motors, they ran submerged.

"If the sun is right, it will reflect off the water," Doc said. "They should lose track of us." To expedite that possibility, he brought them to a dead halt minutes later. They hit bottom, and sat there.

The periscope, when they raised it after a prudent delay, didn't tell them much because it wasn't designed to peer straight up into the sky—but it didn't draw any fire, either.

Thirty minutes later, the three unmarked military planes had not returned. Doc and his men brought the sub to the surface in a stretch of open canal.

Ham had a question: "Assuming—and I think it's a fair assumption under the circumstances—that Max Wood is behind those planes, how did they know that we'd be navigating the Canal by submarine?"

"Our warehouse is well known to our enemies," Doc stated, referring to the dilapidated warehouse on the Hudson River where they housed their planes and boats. "They could have had it watched, and learned we were heading out to sea. Inasmuch as we ran on the surface for most of the trip south, they could easily have tracked us by observation craft. Wood—let's assume it's he—knows we have Tsumi prisoner. He might deduce our only purpose in traveling by submersible would be for a Pacific voyage."

"This must be rather big to involve a plane attack down here," Johnny said with a touch of awe in his tone.

"Bigger than fish, anyway," Monk put in.

"I wonder just *how* big," said Ham Brooks.

Doc Savage, wondering the very same thing, went aft to the tiny cabin where their prisoner was sitting out the voyage. He returned shortly with an unhappy expression.

"What'd he say?" Monk asked.

"He said his name was W. J. Tsumi," Doc said bitterly. He returned to guarding the controls.

They passed through the Pedro Miguel and Miliflores locks without further incident, down to sea level, and ran submerged into the Pacific, without being assessed the standard hefty toll for using the Canal, thanks to Doc's past services. From there on in, the voyage was an agony of monotony or, as Johnny Littlejohn put it, "an interminable excursion of unalleviated tedium." He had gone back to his words, boredom having restimulated his imagination. The bony archaeologist and geologist spent no little time avoiding Monk and Ham, both of whom were in rare agreement that this mystery couldn't really be about missing fish, even though that was the only common thread running through the busy events of the day, but wanted to argue the point, seemingly to death.

On the fourth day out, well north and west of the Hawaiian Islands, they passed the international date line and things became interesting again.

Monk noticed the phenomenon first. He had long before taken to spending his spare hours with his face pressed to various portholes, making absurd faces at the fish who, attracted by the hull lights, had come to investigate him. Nature had given Monk a big mouth not much different from that of a bass—especially when he made fish-breathing shapes with it.

"For crying out loud!" Monk yelled suddenly. "There's a *ton* of fish out there!"

"What did you expect?" Ham remarked acidly. "Fowl? This is the Pacific Ocean, you dope."

"But there's jillions of 'em," Monk argued, exaggerating only a little.

Johnny entered at that point. He took one look out of a porthole and ventured an opinion—at least the others assumed it was an opinion: "A multitudinous aggregation of submarine teleosts bespeaking of questionable origin."

The lanky geologist put his monocle magnifier up to the thick glass and engaged several fish in mutual examination.

Johnny Littlejohn's jaw dropped until his mouth rivaled Monk's in its capaciousness.

He ran and got Doc.

The bronze man regarded the phenomenon of the exodus of passing fish with intent golden eyes. He made—very briefly—a small trilling sound, which ceased immediately. He had to be exceptionally astonished to have done that. The trilling was an old habit of which he'd largely broken himself.

"This is not a normal condition for this portion of the Pacific," he told them tightly. "This region is not known for plentiful sea life. I see species of fish that do not belong this far out to sea."

"Look there, Doc," Johnny said, pointing to a particularly ghastly specimen with a ferocious mouth full of teeth, trailing a kind of natural aerial with glowing white specks on its flank. "Isn't that a deep-sea blackdevil angler?"

Doc nodded. "There are other luminous fish that normally dwell only in abyssal waters. I see goosefish, lanternfish, and the kind of gulper eels that seldom venture up from the unlit depths."

"They seem to be just milling out there," Johnny offered. "I don't see any particular schools. It's just a huge glut of fish, of all types, crowded into this one area."

They stared for almost an hour, taking turns at the controls. Except for whales, and bottom-dwelling crustaceans such as crab and lobster, just about every variety of ocean life known to inhabit the Pacific was congregated around the sub. The sub was bumped a bit, and Doc increased forward speed, because the sheer quantity of marine life began to slow them down.

"Reminds me of the schoolyard from when I was a kid," Monk muttered.

"You still are," Ham couldn't resist adding. "A kid, that is."

They soon got bored with the spectacle, except for Johnny, who monitored the phenomenon and frequently scribbled notes on a pad. Johnny, whose background in archaeology and geology often took him into related fields, was most impressed by the sight. He went forward to confer with Doc Savage frequently. With the result that the two were in a grim mood by the sixth day out.

Monk and Ham were studiously trying to cheat one another at poker when Johnny Littlejohn began making a racket.

"They're gone!" he yelled. "Just like we had stepped into another dimension!"

"We better go see what's ailing old long and bony," Monk sighed, throwing in a losing hand on which he had bet his last twenty.

They found Johnny glued to a porthole. Doc Savage was at his side.

"What now?" Ham demanded.

Doc answered without looking away from the porthole: "We have just passed through a zone of approximately two hundred miles in which the sea life was as thick as flies at an August picnic."

"I know that!"

"Now there are no fish."

"What? Preposterous! Let me see." Ham looked. The sea was a dark blue, even illuminated by the powerful search lamps of the *Helldiver*.

He saw not a solitary fish. Only floating strands of vegetation, such as kelp and seaweed, mixed with the particlelike flotsam of the sea. Even the tiny and plentiful krill were absent.

"Well," he said lamely, "we've just entered a zone where the fish population is less dense."

"That can't make sense, even to you," Monk snorted.

Johnny Littlejohn said it, and the thought sent shivers running down their backs like cold-footed spiders:

"It's as if some phenomenon—or some *thing*—had frightened all the sea life out of this portion of the Pacific."

"That can't be!" Ham said hotly.

Doc said, "If it is—and don't for a minute doubt that such a thing might actually exist—then we are headed straight toward whatever frightened those fish."

Despite the portentous quality of the bronze man's prediction, the remainder of the Pacific crossing was without incident.

They took turns at the controls. Doc used his free time to run tests of the Plum Island water sample. Numerous reagents produced no evidence of the presence of foreign chemicals or other toxic matter. Like the Quincy Bay samples, this one appeared to consist of common ocean water.

On one watch, Doc sent the *Helldiver* running along the bottom. The normally luminous denizens of the deep sea were absent. Likewise, he saw no mollusks or crustaceans. The hull lights showed unusually thick swirls of black specks.

"Plankton?" Johnny wondered aloud, looking at the eddies created as they passed over submerged rocks.

"Those specks are the wrong color for plankton," Doc Savage remarked.

He was concerned enough by this discovery to blow ballast tanks and send the *Helldiver* nosing to the surface.

Doc personally went on deck and lowered a test tube attached to a string over the side. He reeled it back in, half-filled with unsavory-colored brine. Stoppering the tube, Doc returned below.

Monk sent the submarine sinking under the waves once more.

"We're approaching the Kuril Trench," he reported when Doc joined him in the cramped control room. "Want me to take her through?"

"Yes. I want to study this sample. Let me know when we approach Tokyo Bay."

The submarine ghosted through the lifeless waters. Monk increased the angle of the diving planes to negotiate the trench, which was a profoundly deep submarine gash on the ocean floor. It marked the last of deep water and the beginning of the continental shelf around the Islands of Japan.

"Still no fish, eh?" Ham asked when out of sheer boredom he joined Monk at the controls. "Perhaps they are lurking down in this trench beneath us?"

"A lot you know, shyster," Monk squeaked. "The depth's too great for most fish. They can't take the pressure. It would stave in their ribs like a vise. And it won't do this tub much good if I don't keep her level."

Taking the hint, Ham went to a porthole. Lights angling down from the submarine sent weak fans of radiance into the abyss.

"Jove!" Ham breathed.

"What is it, shyster?" Monk demanded. "What do you see?"

"Perhaps it was nothing," Ham said slowly. "But as I was staring into this murk, I fancied I saw something move."

"What do you mean, something? A fish?"

"Too large for a fish."

"Submarine?"

"No, an undersea boat would gleam under the lights."

"Can't be a whale," Monk opined. "They gotta surface every once in a while to get air. Ain't that right, Johnny?"

Johnny Littlejohn had just entered.

"What can't be a whale?" he asked.

"Ham's latest hallucination," Monk said, jerking a thumb in the direction of the dapper lawyer. "He's seeing monsters—or thinks he is."

Johnny elbowed Ham away from the porthole and stared into the murkiness of the Kuril Trench.

"If you stare at one spot long enough, you can discern something colossal move down there," Ham suggested in an awed tone.

Johnny lowered his monocle magnifier.

"An optical oasis," he offered.

"Eh?"

"If you gaze into a dark room without resting your eyes," Johnny explained, "you will experience the identical illusion of movement."

"I say there could be something lurking down there," Ham insisted. "Perhaps some deep-sea creature yet unknown to science. It might have eaten the missing fish."

"Preposterous," Johnny pronounced. "Not even a school of killer whales could consume an oceanful of fish."

"Well, have you a better theory?" Ham snapped.

Johnny said nothing. He returned to his position at the porthole and resumed staring.

Silence settled over the control room. Only the gurgling of water in the ballast tanks and the monotonous toiling of a pump disturbed their thoughts.

V

MYSTIC BAY

The waters approaching Tokyo Bay were peaceful in the way a graveyard on a still day is peaceful. That is, forlornly bare of life, movement, and sound. Once or twice they spotted the baglike otter nets used by Japanese trawlers moving through the waters like blind, foaming ghosts, but that was all.

They saw nothing that might be construed as frightening—even to fish.

"The harbor master says it's O.K. to enter the Port of Tokyo," Ham told Doc, after shutting off the ship-to-shore radio.

"Any problems?" Doc asked. If his experiments with the latest water samples had borne fruit, it was not reflected in his metallic countenance.

"Not for us. The harbor master is part of the American Occupation Forces. But he tells me things are pretty grim in the city since the fish went away."

"How long has this been going on?"

"Three days."

They were running along the surface by this time. Rounding the Boso Peninsula, they entered Sagami Bay, the gateway to the storm shelter of Tokyo Bay. Off to port, the city of Yokohama lay, but even in the morning sun it took some scrutiny to discern what little had been left by incendiary raids during the war. The skyline looked dog-clawed.

"Tokyo isn't much better," Johnny supplied. "We did quite a job there, too. I was here near the end of the war. Almost a hundred square miles were pulverized, and the population was cut in half by casualties and evacuations."

The thought of all that devastation and death held them in the grip of a moody silence until they had anchored and put a collapsible motor launch taken from a storage locker into the water.

"I reckon old W. J. Tsumi will stay put, the amount of ropes I used on him," Monk said. They planned to leave their prisoner on the *Helldiver* to avoid complications.

They berthed near the Central Wholesale Market, next to the Hama Gardens. The Central Wholesale Market was a local fish market where the Tokyo fleet brought their daily catch to be sold. No selling was going on now, however. Trawlers and tuna clippers lay idle. The smell of fish was a nose-offending reek, but it was strictly a residual aroma.

The only fish to be seen were in the shape of colorful paper banners which whipped and rustled from poles lined along the wharfs. They resembled barbaric windsocks.

"Even those paper goldfish look scared," Monk grunted.

"A piscatorial constant owing to their globiform optics," Johnny remarked dryly.

"Is that so?" Monk said vaguely, not understanding any of it.

"He means that all fish wear a frightened look due to their round eyes," Ham supplied. "And I for one agree with him. I think altogether too much has been made of these so-called frightened fish."

"What happened to your underwater monster, shyster?" Monk wanted to know.

Ham colored and lapsed into an embarrassed silence.

Merchants and fishermen congregated along the dock with the sullen silence of men thrown out of work. A few carried placards, and others indulged in some soapbox oratory of the inflammatory variety. Many of the speakers wore red towels—called *tegui*—tied around the tops of their heads.

American Military Police—the backbone of the U.S. Occupation—patrolled the area, tight-lipped and wary.

"I thought MacArthur about had this Occupation thing licked," Monk muttered, returning sullen Japanese stares with glares of his own. Monk won, hands down.

"I knew it was too good to last," Ham put in, "when they hanged Tojo and those other generals for war crimes a few weeks back and there were no demonstrations. Can you imagine what would have happened if the situation were reversed and it was MacArthur's neck in the noose?"

A fight broke out suddenly. The soapbox orator had said something that set the crowd off, and the M.P.s were suddenly descended upon. They fought back with billy clubs and fists. Monk started to wade in. But as suddenly as it had begun, the riot ended, like a boiling kettle after all the water had turned to steam.

The M.P.'s dispersed the crowd with cries of "speedo!" and "hubba-hubba!" They met with no resistance.

The Doc Savage party walked on.

"For the most part," Doc said, "the Japanese population has been cooperative. Once they realized the Occupation only intended to help get this country back on its feet again, Americans were welcomed. There have been no major incidents; in fact, the Japanese have been so polite and accommodating that some Occupation people have been taking unfair advantage of the situation here."

"The missing fish must have changed that," Johnny muttered.

Doc nodded. They kept walking and before long found themselves, much to Monk Mayfair's obvious delight, on *Haromi Dori,* in the Ginza section. The Ginza was Tokyo's garish entertainment district, and a jungle of neon at night. Mostly it was Americans and other foreigners who prowled the wide *Haromi Dori* now, the native Japanese being too preoccupied with putting their lives back in order to indulge much in frivolity.

Monk, ogling a passing kimono-clad girl, remarked absently, "They must be doing a bang-up job of reconstruction to have this part of town cooking again—the Occupation, I mean."

Doc Savage, unimpressed by the district—the bronze man was not much for play—said, "The joint Japanese-Occupation government has made great strides in the last three years, especially after the new American-style Japanese constitution was implemented. Unscrupulous profiteers and the communist element in the Japanese parliament, the *Diet,* have been the major trouble-makers."

They paused to pick up the latest *Stars and Stripes* at a sidewalk magazine stand.

"This isn't good," Johnny said slowly, as he read over Doc's shoulder. "You know how much the Japanese depend upon fish; most of the animal protein in their daily meals comes from food fish. The average Japanese eats ninety-five pounds of it each year. And what they don't eat, they sell abroad. Commercial fishing represents a large portion of the national economy. Well, according to this, the waters east of the Japanese Islands have gone dry—fished out, so to speak. Even after only three days, this is creating a bad economic situation. There have been riots—"

"I think we just saw an example of one," Monk snorted.

"The worst part of it is that communist agitators, who would like to see the American Occupation fall apart, are blaming the situation on the aftereffects of the American bombing attacks. They even hint the phenomenon may be atomic in nature. . . . Doc, is that possible?"

The bronze man looked grim. "The address we want is in the *Bunkyo* ward, north of here. A train will be quickest."

They turned off the *Chuo-Dori,* and found their way to Tokyo Station, lately rebuilt. The train, when it pulled in, was a scabby wreck, with shattered and cracked windows. One car was intact and polished, however, and bore a neat plaque saying: *Reserved for Occupation Forces.* It was a sign of how poorly the Japanese were treated in their own capital city.

Doc and the others nevertheless boarded the reserved car.

It was only about two miles to their destination, but the ride was sobering. All about them, sections of the city lay in ruins. Heaps of rubble rubbed shoulders with wooden shacks. Twisted steel girders formed fantastic rust-scabbed shapes against the flat horizon. Shantytowns were common. An occasional rusty safe sitting in a pile of gray ash was the only testimony that a business establishment had once stood on a particular spot. Still, new apartment housing sprouted here and there in the cold sunlight. In the distance, snowcapped Mount Fuji was visible.

"Sure is a mess," Monk muttered.

"They about had this city rebuilt from the 1923 earthquake when the war started," Johnny said.

"Well," Monk ventured, "they brought that on themselves."

Ham Brooks, who detested untidiness of any type, had his nose buried in *Stars and Stripes*. He looked up, and said in his affected Harvard accent, "Jove! This says that the communists in China have just taken Peiping!"

"Let me see that," Doc demanded. He read the report. A grimness settled over his metallic features.

"Those hammer-and-sickle boys are another bunch that are going to get what's comin' to them someday," Monk predicted levelly.

"This entire corner of the world—Japan included— has become the primary goal of the Soviet Union," Doc told them. "That man who nearly started a riot was a communist agitator. Now that the Russians are known to possess the atom bomb, I'm afraid even the United Nations may not be able to check the spread of Soviet-inspired unrest in Asia."

"I shudder to contemplate the world's future if that happens," Johnny said fervently.

Rattling and wheezing, the train let them off at Ueno Park, not far from the Imperial Tokyo University, now called simply Tokyo University since the Japanese emperor had been stripped of his so-called divinity.

They found themselves in a residential section composed mostly of the one-story paper-and-unpainted-wood dwellings that constitute the average traditional Japanese home. Most of them were intact—or more likely newly built.

"What street are we looking for?" Monk wanted to know.

"They don't go by streets here," Johnny told them, somewhat testily. Johnny tended to be a little intolerant of others' lack of knowledge. "They go by ward, district, block, and house number."

Doc Savage said, "W. J. Tsumi—if that is his true name—kept repeating '2-7, *Asakusa* 1-*chome*, *Bunkyo-Ku*,' which means 'block 2, house 7, subdivision 1 in the *Asakusa* district of the *Bunkyo* ward.'"

"No wonder they lost the war," Monk grumbled. "How do we find it?"

"We ask around."

They did so. The Japanese they encountered were uniformly civil, eagerly supplying directions and in more than one case, offering to guide them to their destination. Doc declined each offer with an equally polite bow.

"These guys are so darned civil it strikes me as suspicious," Monk complained.

"Most Americans here have gotten that mistaken impression," Doc told him. "It is fortunate for the Occupation that submission to authority is ingrained in the average Japanese from birth."

They passed an unnerving number of Japanese men wearing Imperial Army uniforms stripped of all insignia. These individuals were unarmed and, further, seemed to carry about them such an air of dazed defeat that eventually Doc and his men relaxed. All except Monk, who had had several hair-raising brushes with soldiers wearing those same camel-colored uniforms during the war.

"The first one of these guys who starts something, is going to know trouble," Monk promised.

Clutching his sword cane warily, Ham asked Doc, "I thought the Japanese Army had been dissolved."

"It has," Doc told him. "Some of these men wear cast-off uniforms for lack of more suitable clothing. The

Japanese industrial base is a long way from being back on its feet."

"You would think that with a nation to rebuild," Ham noted, "jobs would be plentiful."

"They are," Doc said soberly. "But there are far more Japanese than jobs."

"Sounds like a recipe for revolution," Monk muttered. A sudden thought struck the apish chemist. "Say, Doc. I just realized something. What if these guys are part of a secret army, or something? You know, kinda along the Trojan horse idea."

"Monk has a point," Johnny put in. "Someone had to fly those Zeros we encountered over the Panama Canal."

"Perhaps the answers we seek will be found in the address Tsumi gave us."

The absence of street signs proved daunting. Standing on a street corner, they debated whether or not to split up and conduct separate searches. This afforded Monk and Ham a perfect opportunity to get into an argument.

Finally, Doc accosted a passing young woman wearing a pair of the baggy trousers called a *monpe* which Japanese parents had, in the early days of the Occupation, taken to forcing on their daughters in the—it turned out vain—hope that the trousers would make them unattractive to American soldiers.

"*Konichiwa,*" Doc said by way of greeting.

The pretty Japanese girl returned Doc's salutation with a polite bow.

The bronze man asked the way in deferential Japanese.

"*Ah, so desuka?*" she murmured. Then she pointed west and spoke so rapidly that Johnny, standing nearby, had trouble following the exchange.

After she had finished, Doc thanked her by saying *"Arigato,"* and bowing once.

This enabled them to narrow their quest down to a single one-story house. It appeared deserted, but on a raw blustery day such as this, that might not be true. The lack of high buildings to serve as windbreaks contributed greatly to the discomfort of being outdoors.

"Well?" Ham prodded.

"There's no point in rushing headlong into any more darkened rooms," Doc said. He reached into a coat pocket and pulled from it a container of small capsules. "These," he told the others, "contain our usual anæsthetic gas, but in a stronger mixture. In other words, it won't neutralize itself for at least five minutes. Have you all your gas masks?"

Monk, Ham, and Johnny each pulled from his clothing a simple type of protective mask consisting, simply, of cellophane sacks worn over the head and closed at the neck by elastic bands.

These were good only for two or three minutes at a time, but probably that would be all they would need.

"We don't know what we are in for," Doc reminded them, "so be prepared for anything."

The others unlimbered compact weapons with drum magazines—special machine pistols they always carried, which fired so-called mercy bullets. Doc personally never carried the guns, however. He believed that a man tended to grow reliant upon weapons, the loss of which would render him psychologically unprepared to deal with adverse situations.

They approached the house cautiously, and dropped to the ground next to a large sliding door. All traditional Japanese houses were built along the same lines, so they knew this door led into what passed for a parlor.

Doc eased the door open a crack and flipped a

handful of the capsules inside. These broke and volatilized instantaneously.

They retreated to a safe distance and waited.

Doc signaled them with hand signs. Donning their gas masks, they plunged in, their steady breathing making the cellophane bladders of the masks rhythmically change shape.

"Empty!" Johnny announced, after a thorough search.

It was disconcerting, but true. The house they had traveled half across the world to investigate was indeed deserted.

"Someone's been living here, though," Ham decided after checking the kitchen. "This *hibachi* has seen recent use."

"What next?" was homely Monk's question.

Doc, finishing his examination, said, "Something may yet turn up at this location, but not if we all camp out here. Monk, you will remain. Contact us with your pocket radio transceiver if anyone else shows up."

"What about the rest of you guys?" Monk wanted to know.

"We will look into the mystery of the vanished fish."

The desk clerk at the Imperial Hotel on *Ginza Dori* was telling them: "*Sa, chotto muzukashii desu, ne,*" which meant that securing rooms for them would be difficult.

Doc countered that plea by saying, in Japanese, "Difficult, but not impossible, eh?"

The desk clerk professed not to know what was meant.

Doc said, "Never mind," and went to make a call to the Tokyo headquarters of the Supreme Commander Allied Powers. Not many minutes later, the desk clerk received a call from SCAP that caused him to change his tune. Like all major hotels, even when booked solid, the establishment kept a room or two in readiness for unexpected visiting dignitaries.

Evidently Doc and his party suddenly qualified for that category, because they were promptly given a vacant suite of rooms on the top floor. Once ensconced in these quarters, Doc Savage began making telephone calls and issuing orders to his men.

Not long after, Ham and Johnny brought the trunk containing the sedated W. J. Tsumi up to their suite. At Doc's suggestion, they had gone back to the *Helldiver* to retrieve him.

"Where do you want this fellow, Doc?" Ham inquired, after they unceremoniously dropped the trunk on the floor.

The bronze man came over to the trunk, unlatched it, and exposed W. J. Tsumi's fear-struck, toadlike face. His wrists were bound together high on his chest, and his mouth was stuffed with a handkerchief whose green gaudiness proclaimed itself to be Monk's property.

Doc undid the gag.

"Are you ready to talk?" he asked.

"*Iiee*," Tsumi said tersely, shaking his head stubbornly.

"For your information, we are in Tokyo," Doc told him. "The situation is very bad here. All the fish have fled the waters. No one seems to understand why, and the people are frightened. Care to enlighten us on Max Wood's role in this?"

W. J. Tsumi absorbed Doc's words. The defiance leaked from his expression. His eyes were clear now, the truth serum having worn off. A variety of expressions—chiefly puzzlement and concern—chased themselves across his unlovely features.

Finally, Tsumi declined Doc's offer with the more

polite Japanese term for no. "*Chigau, domo,*" he whispered. His voice was subdued.

Monk Mayfair made a show of cracking his rusty knuckles as he said, "Want me to work him over, Doc?"

"No," Doc said thoughtfully. He restored the gag. Then he checked Tsumi's bonds for tightness, loosening them a little to alleviate any hampering of blood circulation.

Noting this, Monk Mayfair scratched his head. He seemed about to speak up, when his attention was drawn to the windows.

Down on the street, a chorus of shouting reached all the way up to their suite.

"*Wa-Shoi! Wa-Shoi! Wa-Shoi!*"

Ham Brooks went to the window and shoved it up. He poked his well-tonsured head out.

"Looks like a parade," he mused. "What's that they're shouting?"

Joining him, Johnny offered a different opinion.

"That is no parade," he pronounced, "but a trade union demonstration. They seem to be striking."

"I see a lot of those red towels," Monk added. "That jabber they're shouting, what's it mean?"

"Nothing, really," Johnny told him. "It is a bit like our own rah-rah—just a sound conducive for mass shouting."

One eye on Tsumi, Monk wondered, "I say we shake some facts out of our friend Tsumi here."

"Keep an eye on him," Doc said abruptly, striding toward the door, "but do not harm him in any way."

"Where you goin'?" Monk squeaked.

The door closed on the bronze man's broad back.

Doc Savage left the hotel by the back way, thus avoiding the demonstration. Its noise followed him all the way down to the waterfront. Until now, the hectic nature of this adventure had not given the bronze man time to investigate the phenomenon of the vanished fish. He fully intended to do so now.

Doc guided his collapsible motor launch out onto Tokyo Bay, and cut the motor. After dropping anchor, he stripped to a pair of black silk shorts he always wore under his street clothes and plunged in. He wore a small diving "lung."

The bay was bone-chilling, and the bronze man knew that even his constitution would not stand an extended immersion. He kept an eye on the luminous dial of his watch.

It was the eeriest swim of Doc Savage's life. In an area known for its teeming sea life, the ocean was a watery tomb. Virtually nothing swam under the surface. Above, fishing boats of various types trawled aimlessly. Below, nothing moved. It was as if, Doc thought, he had dived into some liquid element other than water, or into another realm, one inimical to life in any form. Doc grabbed fistfuls of cold brine and examined his hand. not even plankton, the chief source of food for most finny varieties of fish, floated by.

Doc broke the surface and removed his lung.

Above his head, the Japanese species of sea gulls, called *Yuri-kamoune*, circled, vulturelike. Their ghoulish hungry cries hardly induced a soothing feeling. Over on a drifting chunk of wood, the bronze man spied one of the gulls greedily eating one of its fellows— something that type of bird only did when it was desperate.

Doc dived again.

This time, he found something.

Near the sunken remains of a Mitsubishi 96 "Karigane" MK II, which had probably been shot down during one of the incendiary raids, Doc found a *tako tsubo*—a crockery octopus trap. It shook like an oversized Mexican jumping bean. He brought it to the surface.

Peering inside, Doc discovered a small octopus trapped in the pot. It was a livid scarlet color. It flopped and floundered and slashed the air rapidly with its tiny beak, obviously in need of oxygen.

Doc dunked the pot, with the octopus inside. The mollusk was no less agitated back in its own element. In fact, it declined to evacuate the earthenware trap. Its behavior was wild—and something about the way it flung its ropy tentacles about the rim sent a brief chill up the bronze man's spine, one that was not produced by the icy waters.

Doc reached in and extracted the octopus. It squirmed in his metallic fist. As an experiment, he let the flame-colored creature go. It sank. Doc followed it down.

The octopus, its almost-human eyes wide as half dollars, expanded its bladderlike sac of a head in preparation for expelling a jet of water through its siphon. It squirted itself a good ten yards, swirling its tentacles around, and took in more water. This time it shot closer to thirty yards, but in another direction.

Doc swam after it, curious. Normally, the octopus was a gentle, harmless denizen of the deep, one inclined to slither into sheltering coral and grottos when threatened. But this particular specimen was exhibiting all the symptoms of uncontrolled panic.

Gulping water that swelled its humped bulb of a head, the octopus sent itself shooting through the water, its bundles of tentacles trailing behind like a stringy old mop. It flung itself in one direction, then another, often reversing itself.

Doc kept his distance. Noticing that its burning coloration was reddening with each exertion.

Eventually, the creature tired. It squirted a sudden

cloud of billowing black ink. Current dissipated the cloud very quickly. The octopus struggled to the surface, as if seeking shelter. Doc followed.

The creature never made it. It was as if its many tentacles were being pulled to the surface by invisible strings and the strings had suddenly been cut. The delicate tentacle tips, reaching upward, lost their straining quality. They wilted, and the mollusk expelled a flurry of bubbles all at once.

It floated to the surface. It was dead. Slowly, its livid scarlet hue drained away, leaving a natural slate-gray coloration.

There was a small cubicle on the *Helldiver* which served as a makeshift lab area. Doc was performing a dissection of the octopus there.

He cut away a section of the mollusk's head and exposed its major organs. They were all intact but for the hearts. It possessed three of them. The hearts, Doc was astounded to learn, had burst.

He next extracted a bit of fluid from another organ and ran some chemical tests. He was not surprised when the tests told him that the octopus's adrenaline production had been unusually high at the time it expired. Its livid coloration, he knew, was a natural response to danger and certain other external stimuli.

The octopus seemed to have been healthy otherwise.

It had simply died of *fear*.

Doc Savage's eerie trilling permeated the tiny cubicle.

VI

BRONZE MAN GONE

Doc Savage was in the middle of testing the third
seawater sample from Tokyo Bay when Johnny came on
the radio.

*"Monk's in trouble. Listen on your pocket trans-
ceiver."*

Doc switched the gadget on. The tiny radio was
one he invented, and which Doc and his associates used
to communicate with one another when more powerful
sets were not handy. It operated on the U.H.F. band off
a tiny self-contained battery, and utilized peanut tubes
for compactness.

Monk was saying in a tight voice: *"There's two of
them at least. I got the main door covered, but I think
one of them is trying to sneak around and come up from
behind."*

"Monk—this is Doc. Try to take them out with
your mercy gun. Repeat: Endeavor to hold them there.
We're on our way . . . Ham—Johnny. You hear me? Get
out to the *Bunkyo* ward as fast as you can. I'll be there
directly."

"Check," Johnny said, and switched off.

The bronze man turned off the Bunsen burner he'd
been using to heat the seawater sample, and kept an
ear cocked to the small radio. Monk's heavy breathing

was the only sound for several minutes. Doc stoppered the seawater sample. He had not been making any progress with his tests. The first two samples had contained ordinary ocean brine, unusual only in its utter absence of life. There had only been the minute corpses of microscopic sea animals—krill and plankton—in quantities that might be found in ordinary seawater. Incredibly, whatever had driven the larger fish from the Tokyo Bay area had similarly affected even the smallest forms of life.

Otherwise, the samples gave no clue to the influence which had seemingly filtered all life from the sea.

A moaning bull-fiddle roar jumped from the pocket radio. It was Monk's machine pistol discharging continuously. It ceased abruptly, then the homely chemist came on the air:

"Doc! They—yeoow!" There was a dull clattery sound, as if Monk's radio had fallen to the floor. Feet whetted nearby. Then, came various scufflings and blows.

"Monk!" Doc called.

Monk's voice, when Doc Savage heard it next, had a far, muffled sound which didn't disguise the evident astonishment in his tone:

"Doc! You'll never believe this! It's Mah—"

The next sound told the bronze man the radio had been destroyed, probably by a heavy foot.

The *basha*—or taxi—was over twenty years old and, in its day, had probably been an excellent automobile. Now it was a pitted, smoking nightmare which had been made over to run on wood. A contraption attached to the radiator belched the sooty smoke. It wasn't luxurious, but it traveled, and it was the best Ham Brooks and Johnny Littlejohn could manage under the circumstances, which were not good.

They were rattling through the *Kanda* district when

Monk's last message came over their pocket transceivers. Johnny urged the driver to go faster. The latter worthy did his best, but Ham and Johnny were convinced afterward that he put the greater part of his energy into apologies, not forward motion.

"I fear a deficit of temporal juxtaposition," Johnny moaned.

"If by that you mean you don't think we'll reach Monk in time, I'm afraid you're right." Ham vented a choice oath and seemed about to break his sword cane in his white-knuckled hands. Monk meant a lot to him, though he would never admit that publicly.

What seemed like hours later, they reached the house in the *Bunkyo* ward.

In his excitement, Ham paid the driver twenty *yen*—almost double the fare even with Japanese inflation—and the driver's grateful *"Arigato, arigato"* followed them to the house. The door was open.

They found, variously, a shoved-aside screen, signs of a struggle, and Monk's radio in pieces on the *genka*, or porch—but no Monk. Or anyone else for that matter.

Ham did find a heavy iron candlestick, called a *te-shoku*, which was badly bent.

"Looks like they brained Monk with this item," Ham said, hefting it. He looked sick at the thought.

"Nothing we can do here," Johnny said glumly.

They settled down to await the arrival of Doc Savage.

No one had seen anything, a quick check of all houses on the block by Doc and Johnny indicated. The Japanese were, as always, excessively polite and helpful, but the hint of trouble in the neighborhood involving Americans plainly gnawed at their natural willingness to help. Trouble with Americans usually meant summoning the M.P.s, and no Japanese cared to be involved with that kind of situation.

"Maybe we should bring the Occupation in on this," Ham suggested hopefully.

They were back at the deserted house, and Doc was combing the grounds with a powerful flashlight of the hand-operated generator type. It sprayed light of almost calcium whiteness through the early dusk and, in addition, could power a small radio or detonate explosive charges. It was one of the many gadgets he had invented, and which were a hobby with him.

At Doc's direction, Johnny and Ham were giving the house interior a good going-over.

"There's something strange about this place," Johnny was saying, as he poked at the remnant of a fire in the center of the main room of the house. This held a square pit in its center, called a *ro*, where charcoal was burned for heat.

"I'll say it's strange," Ham remarked grimly.

"No. Something is missing. . . . Here!"

With a bony digit, Johnny indicated a little nook in one wall.

"What of it?"

"It's a *tokonoma*—the alcove where the Japanese traditionally set a flower arrangement and a decorative scroll they call a *kalemono*, which is sort of a shrine to family and ancestors. But there is no scroll or flowers."

"So?" Ham asked skeptically.

"No Japanese house would be without a scroll," Johnny said slowly, "unless it was owned by a foreigner. I'd better go tell Doc; this may be significant."

Ham remained indoors, examining a ghastly little *bonsai* tree which sat in its pot like a soul that had been reduced to twisted charcoal tentacles. It was an example of what passed for beauty in the Japanese culture, Ham reflected, which doesn't say very much for the

Japanese concept of beauty. There were no chairs, only *tatami* mats arranged on the floor for seating purposes. Ham, conscious of the knifelike crease in his trousers, eschewed using these mats for their intended purpose.

Ham's musing were rudely intruded upon by a sharp squeal of an automobile quitting the area in a hurry. Somewhere, Johnny Littlejohn howled something entirely unintelligible. Ham fought the *shoshi* screen which had gotten caught in its grooves, and dropped into the garden, nearly colliding with Johnny in the increasing murk.

"What's happening?" Ham demanded. "Where's Doc?"

Johnny, for once, had difficulty with his words, even though they were small ones. He tried to speak three times, but astonishment tangled up whatever he had to say.

Ham shook him violently, repeated: *"Where's Doc?"*

The gaunt archæologist took a deep breath and swept his long hair back from his forehead with both hands.

"Doc got into a car, and it took off!"

"What do you mean, he got into a car?"

"I—I had just come out," Johnny said breathlessly. "A car pulled up next to Doc. He went over to it and started speaking with the driver. They had no sooner exchanged a couple of words when Doc got in and they drove off."

"That's crazy!" Ham said excitedly. "Why would Doc do that? He wouldn't just up and leave us here!"

"That isn't the crazy part," Johnny said strangely. *"The driver was a woman!"*

VII

WAR?

"Let's take this from the top," Ham Brooks said in his best courtroom manner. He was pacing up and down their hotel suite, and had been for the last hour, ever since he and Johnny Littlejohn had returned from a futile search of the *Helldiver*. They didn't find Doc Savage aboard the sub—or anywhere else for that matter. "Perhaps we can make some sense out of this if we talk it out."

Ham didn't really believe this, but he was nervous and disconcerted. Doc Savage's behavior, as reported by Johnny, was not like that of the bronze man. Doc simply wouldn't run out on his friends in a situation like the one at the Japanese house, Ham reasoned. Especially with a strange woman. Or *was* she a strange woman?

"Are you certain the woman in the car wasn't Celia Adams?" he inquired of Johnny.

"Positive."

"But you say you didn't see her clearly; it was too dark. Then it *might* have been her, mightn't it?"

"Stop grasping at straws!" Johnny shot back. "It was not Celia; I just didn't see her clearly enough to get details. And Doc wasn't kidnaped, either. Don't get that idea. He didn't act as if he were being threatened, and I observed no weapon."

Ham threw up his hands. "It doesn't make sense! No woman can pick up Doc Savage just like that."

"Let's try this from another angle," Johnny ventured. He spun his lapel monocle by its ribbon and struck a learned pose, like a lecturer, which he actually was. For years, Johnny had headed the natural science department of a prestigious university.

"Something—we do not know what—has so terrified the fish in the waters on this side of Japan that they have fled far into the Pacific. This same agency may or may not be operating off the Massachusetts coast—and elsewhere, for all we know at present."

"What we know at present," Ham said bitterly, "is damn little."

Johnny cleared his throat and went on: "We were dragged into this by some strange goings-on in New York by certain plotters who were concerned that Doc knew something about this fish mystery because they made a big fuss over a silver fish—in each case the fish was silver. That point may be important."

"Perhaps there is a clue in the varieties of fish involved," Ham suggested.

"Doubtful," Johnny returned crisply. "The species involved in the altercation at that Greenwich Village restaurant was a common butterfish. I myself looked into the particulars. Later, the same individual became agitated at the sight of a grocery-store carp and postcards bearing the likeness of a mounted swordfish. Those three varieties are as unlike as fish can be. The butterfish is small and draws its sustenance from the seafloor, as does the carp. Such fish are called *benthos*. On the other hand, the swordfish is pelagic, which means it lives and feeds near the surface."

"What about the porcupinelike-fish drawing outside our headquarters? The puffer. What kind was that one?"

"A bottom feeder, sustaining itself on crabs and other invertebrates. It possesses the remarkable ability to puff itself up in order to frighten away predators. When it does this, its spines protrude. Although found off both coasts in the United States, it is common in Japanese waters as well, where it is called *fugu*. Puffers are highly prized as a Japanese delicacy, despite their lethal toxicity."

"Their what?"

"Puffers," Johnny said pointedly, "are poisonous."

"But you say they're a delicacy," Ham blurted.

"Correct. Properly prepared, they can be eaten. But if the chef makes a mistake in preparation, and the poisonous portions are consumed, death usually results."

"Then the fish specimens are meaningless," Ham stated. "They have nothing in common."

"Untrue," Johnny retorted. "In every case, the fish in question were described by witnesses as appearing frightened. Obviously that is the key."

"It's maddening," Ham moaned. The illogic of the situation had gotten his natty goat.

Johnny continued: "All of this ties in with something an ichthyologist named Baker Eastland has or knows and with a sinister man named Max Wood."

"Whatever it's all about," Ham inserted, "it is not small. Those Zeros which attacked us over the Panama Canal are proof of that. And then there's our Japanese friend, Tsumi, in the next room."

Johnny abruptly lost his professorial pose, not to mention the color in his face. "Wait a minute. Those Zeros! Everyone knows the Jap military apparatus has been dismantled. But suppose there are arms caches scattered in different locales."

Ham started. "My God! Are you saying what I think you are? It's incredible."

"It is a fact that a formal peace treaty between America and Japan has yet to be signed even now— over three years after the surrender," Johnny said reasonably.

"It's too wild. Japan is beaten. They don't have the resources. They aren't about to reopen hostilities."

"But they might if their present rate of economic recovery is interrupted," Johnny countered. "This fish business may be a ploy to incite the overthrow of the American-instituted constitutional government here. Everyone knows that the *Diet* is full of communist sympathizers and at this point is not very stable. It would not take much to bring the whole government down, especially with the Japanese people in a state of confusion over the Emperor's renunciation of his divinity."

Ham stood up purposely. "I think it's time we took this to SCAP."

Johnny shook his shaggy head. "No, if Doc wanted to bring MacArthur's office into this, he would have by now. Our best move," he finished grimly, "is to give our friend, W. J. Tsumi, a thorough going-over."

"That won't be necessary," a controlled voice said from the door. "Tsumi is on our side."

"Doc!" Ham and Johnny chorused.

Doc Savage entered the suite. His bronze features wore strain and a powdered-metal pallor in equal measure, but otherwise he looked no worse for his experience— whatever it might have been.

"Good Lord, Doc, we've been worried sick about you," Ham ejaculated. "Where have you been all this time?"

"Having dinner."

"Having—?"

Then the woman stepped into the room. She was tall, dark-haired, and radiant, although pallor, too, had worked into the composed softness of her face, turning it a little to the hue of bone. She was nonetheless beautiful in a contained way as Doc Savage introduced her.

"I believe you and Ham have already had the pleasure," the bronze man said quietly. "Johnny Littlejohn, this is Seryi Mitroff."

"*Kak vahse zdarovye?*" Seryi said smilingly in fluent Russian.

Johnny, taken aback by the colloquial "How are you doing?" got his words tangled up again. His Russian "I am fine" was a croak.

Ham was speechless, a condition not greatly improved upon when Monk Mayfair, a bandage swathing his nubbin skull, entered next, followed by a hulking oaf of a man whom Doc proceeded to introduce in a tone usually reserved for proud fathers at their daughters' weddings.

"And this is Mahli, her cousin."

Mahli nodded his ugly head. He did not look comfortable. None of them did. Monk was especially quiet.

Johnny and Ham exchanged looks.

"Seryi? Isn't she the one who—?" Johnny undertoned to Ham.

Ham nodded. "She's the one, all right."

Johnny fell silent. He had not been involved in the hair-raising adventure behind the Iron Curtain, almost a year ago, in which Doc, Monk, and Ham had stolen into Soviet Russia to learn whether that nation had achieved the atom bomb. In the course of that mission, they had encountered Seryi and her cousin, Mahli, who had helped them out—and who had nearly died with them in front of a Soviet firing squad. Seryi had made a remarkable dent in Doc Savage's ordinarily unsusceptible demeanor in a very short time—and the attraction had been unmistakably mutual.

Seryi and Mahli had been left behind in Russia at the conclusion of that mission, intending to carry on against the Stalin regime, which they violently opposed. Doc and his aides had never expected to see the pair again.*

After the introductions had been concluded, Doc said, "There appears to have been a misunderstanding, which, given the circumstances, might be forgiven."

"What's going on, Doc?" Ham asked a little wildly, and noted with a panicky frown that Seryi Mitroff had taken the bronze man's arm, and he seemed not to mind. She looked up at him and approval shone in her intelligent eyes, but in back of that light there was a haunted look.

"As I say," Doc repeated, "a slight misunderstanding." He turned to Johnny Littlejohn, saying, "Johnny, why don't you release Mr. Tsumi?"

Johnny did so, and W. J. Tsumi entered the room. Confusion overspread his tea-colored features when he spied Seryi and her oafish-looking cousin.

Seryi demanded something of him in Russian.

"*Kare no hara ga yomenai,*" W. J. Tsumi said, regarding the bronze man.

"What did they say?" Ham asked Johnny.

"She asked him why he had not explained his mission to Doc Savage, and he said, literally, 'I could not read his stomach,' a Japanese expression which translates as 'I couldn't guess his intentions,' more or less."

"You mean this Max Wood and his outfit are on our side?" Ham demanded. "That doesn't make sense."

"It's not that way," Doc told him. "Mr. Tsumi is

---

*The Red Spider

working with Seryi. He was a plant in the Wood
organization. We were fortunate—or unfortunate, depending on how this affair winds up—to inadvertently
capture him. The address he gave us while under the
truth drug's influence was that of the house Seryi was
using as her Tokyo headquarters while she investigated
this thing on her end. She and Mahli happened to
return while Monk was waiting there and, uncertain as
to his identity and intentions, captured him."

"An explanatory narrative producing cerebral verti-
go," Johnny said, by way of saying Doc's explanation
made him dizzy.

"What language is that one speaking, Clark?" Seryi
asked Doc Savage.

At Seryi's familiar use of the bronze man's first
name, three sets of jaws—Monk's, Ham's, and Johnny's—
dropped as if unhinged, and her question never did get
answered.

Instead, Doc Savage told them, "I think we had all
better sit down for this."

They all sat, conscious of the undertone of concern
in Doc's voice. The bronze man didn't begin at once.
He spent a few moments, assisted by the beautiful
Seryi, in getting a warm blaze going in the fireplace at
one end of the room. Lack of fuel in postwar Japan
made fireplaces commonplace, even in the best of
hotels. The bronze man, his three aides realized, was
less concerned with the fire than with composing his
thoughts for whatever he had to say.

Monk had taken a seat between Ham and Johnny.

"What on earth is going on?" Ham whispered.

"Beats me," the apish chemist rumbled. "I was
camped out, waiting for something, when I heard someone prowling outside that paper house. I went to
investigate, and that Mahli jumped me. We didn't
recognize each other at first, on account of the dark.

Before I could get a warning to you guys, he was all over me. I would have nailed him, too," Monk finished ruefully, "but something conked me on the head."

"Candlestick," Johnny said.

"What?"

"You were hit on the head by a candlestick."

"Huh. That Seryi babe musta done it, then. I'm not sure I trust her all that much." Which was nothing if not a prejudicial statement. Monk had no admiration for brainy women, of which Seryi Mitroff was one.

"Then what?" asked Ham.

"I woke in a shack somewhere near Shiba Park, not far from here, with that Mahli holdin' a club over me. Next thing I know, Doc and the Russian babe show up, fresh from a cozy little dinner, as I get it. Doc tells me to relax and slaps a bandage on my head. We all pile in a car and here we are."

"That's it?" Ham questioned.

"Unless you count the goofy way Doc has been actin' toward Seryi."

"I'd say the young lady has gotten her hooks in Doc, all right," Johnny suggested, one eye on the too-familiar way Seryi Mitroff helped Doc Savage stir at the burning fireplace logs with an ornate poker.

"Hold onto your hats," Monk warned, low-toned. "Unless Doc is pullin' a stunt, this is definitely a two-way street. It was 'Clark, this' and 'Seryi, that' all during the ride over."

Silence fell over the trio.

"Doc is up to something," Johnny finally said.

That particular subject was promptly forgotten as Doc and Seryi rejoined them—sitting comfortably close to one another, they all noticed in alarm—and launched into as unsettling a speech as ever raised their collective hair on end.

"What I have to say is directed at my three aides, who are still very much in the dark regarding this affair," he began.

"This will be much clearer if I first review the present world situation, which has a direct bearing on the matter. As you all know, the more than three years since the last war have been anything but peaceful. I refer specifically to the hoggish division of conquered nations among the Allies, and especially to the fact that Soviet Russia appears bent upon absorbing as much of Europe and Asia as it can gobble up."

Mahli grunted. He stood with his brawny arms folded like an idol in stone.

"In this year of 1949, in this very area of the world, the influence of communist sympathizers and agitators is as strongly felt as Nazism and Fascism was in Europe in the years immediately preceding the war. Recent events make it clear that Communism may take all of China, and that Korea and Indo-China are likewise threatened. Even here, in American-controlled Japan, Soviet-backed agents have infiltrated the Japanese Diet. In short, this entire portion of the world is facing the prospect of falling under the Iron Curtain."

Doc paused to let the gist of his speech—it was beginning to sound exactly like one—sink in.

"This movement is obviously a coordinated one," he continued. "There is no doubt whatsoever that the present Russian regime is back of it. But it is also true that that regime is not eager to engage in another major war, which is why subversion is the main tool being employed toward achieving its greedy ends. It is not the case, as Johnny suggested earlier, that Japan is planning another war against the United States. Far from it. The current Japanese government is eager to get on with the business of reconstruction and economic recovery."

W. J. Tsumi, who had been untied and had stood rubbing his chafed wrists throughout, nodded vigorously.

"In short," Doc said, "the aim of our friends behind the Iron Curtain is to wrest control of this corner of the world through sheerly political means. Even the squabbling going on between the nationalists in China and the communists is essentially political. That is, it is strictly an internal affair."

A log snapped sparks and split with a mushy crack. The fitful light it cast sent wavering shadows over the faces of the assembled group.

"We have reason to believe, however," Doc Savage resumed, "that there is a single genius manipulating these political activities. One man who controls not only the communist agitators throughout Asia—but also controls the Kremlin."

Doc stopped to lever the split log back onto the andirons. His features were deceptively calm when he returned to his chair.

"That man is Max Wood."

Shocked silence greeted Doc Savage's quiet statement. Monk, Ham, and Johnny sat stonily, letting the idea sink in.

Doc continued: "Wood's plans, as Seryi has outlined them to me, are approaching fruition."

"This is true, just as Clark says," Seryi added. "My cousin and I first heard about this Max Wood slightly less than a year ago. We investigated, and discovered that his tentacles had extended throughout the Soviet, even into the very inner halls of the Kremlin. Our work brought us here to Japan, where we made contact with our friend, Tsumi, who is a former member of Japan's espionage apparatus jailed during the war for opposing the militarist clique. He agreed to infiltrate the Max

Wood organization for us. From information he piped to us, we knew a major attack upon Japan's very economic and political structure was being readied, but we had no details. Then, part of the Max Wood organization went to America, and Tsumi with them. And we have heard nothing since."

Speaking fair English, W. J. Tsumi broke into the narration: "I was only able to learn what you all know now: That Max Wood had obtained something which affected sea life, and was prepared to attack my country through its dependence upon its fishing industry. But he feared a man he called Doc Savage, and sent myself and some others to America to learn if this man had knowledge of the plan, and to kill him if he did. There we joined up with an American group of his agents, who were searching for a man named Baker Eastland. The rest you know."

"Who is this Max Wood?" Johnny questioned. "What is his goal?"

W. J. Tsumi told him: "He is what we call in Japan, a man with a black stomach—a very bad man, a monster. I know only that he is a scientist, that he has men and military equipment stationed all over the world, and that he lusts for power."

"That explains the Zeros that attacked us," Monk put in.

"Max Wood is a complete mystery," Seryi said. "No one knows where he came from, or the nature of his ultimate goals. We do know that he could very well trigger a new war by his reckless actions, and may even be bent upon doing so."

"Indeed," Doc Savage said. He looked from Seryi's concerned face to address the assembled group. "You can see the scope of this thing. The four of us have been through a great deal in the course of our careers. We have been all over the world, and have fought in virtually every corner of it for the things we hold dear—principles like justice, freedom, and a peaceful future for mankind. These beliefs may sound old-fashioned in this modern, war-cynical world, but they are real; they have held us together in common cause as long as we have known each other."

Doc Savage stood up. "Make no mistake about it: *Max Wood is the greatest single threat to mankind since Adolf Hitler.*"

VIII

JUNK SINISTER

The quickest route to the other side of Japan by submarine was by steaming south through a strait between the main Japanese island of Honshu and the smaller Shikoku and Kyushu isles to the stretch of open water between Korea and Nippon—known as the Sea of Japan. Dawn found the *Helldiver* cutting through that strait with the leveled city of Hiroshima well off to starboard and out of sight, but hanging in their minds like a dark portent of the future.

Doc Savage had suggested that they join forces with Seryi Mitroff and her companions—an idea which met with no great favor with Monk, Ham, and Johnny— and head first to the Sea of Japan on the theory that, as the fishing was only beginning to suffer there according to radio reports, whatever agency was at work might still be operating and subject to investigation.

Doc's three aides were not exactly enamored of Seryi Mitroff. The bronze man gave every indication of liking and trusting her, but they could all remember occasions in which he had allowed individuals to string along on an investigation, only to have it come out that those individuals were among the guilty. They wondered if that might not be the case here.

It was Monk Mayfair who took Ham and Johnny

aside and asked aloud the question which had been gnawing at their minds for hours: "You don't suppose Doc has fallen in love, do you?"

"It doesn't seem possible," Ham mused, "but it certainly is beginning to look that way. They haven't been out of each other's sight since Tokyo."

"I still say Doc is up to something," Johnny countered.

"Could be, but I seem to recollect this electricity started back in Moscow last year."

"That's true," Ham stated firmly. "And I, for one, cannot ever recall a woman affecting Doc so deeply as Seryi did, even then."

"I still don't trust her," Monk said. "Or her friends."

"But what if it *is* true," Ham prompted.

"What if it is? Doc has never criticized our interest in babes—much."

"But isn't this Seryi a communist?" Ham asserted.

Monk started. "I hadn't thought of that angle. I don't know. Is she? She hates the current Soviet government and its terror tactics, but that doesn't mean she isn't a party member."

"Doc in love with a Communist Party member?" Johnny said. "Rubbish! He wouldn't. It's unthinkable."

"I haven't noticed that love promotes much thinking," Monk told him. "Besides, she might be Doc's type—the brainy variety, you know?"

"I don't know," Johnny muttered. "I always thought that if Doc were to settle down and get married, he would pick that Mayan princess, Monja, the one who lives in the lost valley where we get all our gold." Johnny was referring to a remote valley in the Central American country of Hidalgo, where dwelled the last of the Mayan Indians, the guardians of Doc's treasure trove of gold, which he used to finance his work. They seldom visited the Valley of the Vanished, as it was called, these days.

"Yeah," Monk added. "I've often thought that myself. Princess Monja has been in love with Doc for years, and I know he likes her, too. But you guys know Doc—he's woman-proof! And besides, he's always said that his life was too dangerous to include a wife. He has too many enemies."

"I get the impression that Seryi's life is no picnic, either," Ham said soberly.

"Blazes!" Monk squeaked. "It could be true, at that, couldn't it?"

Even Johnny was shaken by Monk's outburst. He asked: "If Doc gets married, what will it mean to our excitement-chasing?"

"I don't know," Ham said. "But I do know if we don't stop Max Wood's devilish scheme, a lot more than our excitement-chasing will be over."

The *Helldiver* ran along the surface of the Inland Sea in order not to be mistaken for an enemy submarine. Doc had cleared his presence in the area with SCAP headquarters in Tokyo, but refused to divulge his mission. A heated exchange had ensued, with the bronze man emerging victorious simply by cutting off all radio communication and getting under way. They were not challenged.

When they reached the Sea of Japan, Doc gave the order to submerge, and for several minutes there was only the rush and gurgle of the buoyancy tanks taking on water while the *Helldiver* achieved neutral buoyancy and sank slowly. The surface Diesels were cut and electric motors took over, their insistent sound masked by the laboring air conditioners as they greedily gobbled carbon dioxide and replenished the oxygen.

"According to the latest information," Doc Savage

told them, looking up from the radio set, "fishermen on this side of the islands are now reporting a scarcity of catches well north of here. We will head for that area first."

The hours passed. Doc, Monk, Ham, and Johnny busied themselves with the operation of the old submarine, trimming tanks often to maintain a constant depth. Seryi, her cousin, Mahli, and W. J. Tsumi, unfamiliar with submarine navigation, and because of the cramped confines, stayed well aft listening to Japanese radio broadcasts.

Seryi came forward only once, to announce that severe rioting had broken out in Tokyo, Yokohama, and several other large cities over the lack of eatable fish. The *Diet* was in special session, and MacArthur was planning to broadcast a special plea for restraint from his headquarters in the *Dai-Ichi* Building.

"It is very, very bad," Seryi finished. "We may already be too late."

That did not exactly promote a festive mood.

Afternoon found the *Helldiver* encountering numerous schools of fish traveling south. There were bluefin tuna, sardine, and bonito. Once, a boat dragging a bell-shaped purse seine net snared an entire school of bluefin tuna, and they watched the net being drawn into a circle around the school by a smaller skiff, close up like a gigantic drawstring purse, and disappear toward the surface with its active catch.

The schools multiplied as they pressed northward and gradually the seas were choked with fish, tuna and herring predominating, all fleeing south, and all, Monk was convinced—although this was debatable—wearing expressions of utter terror.

"Well, something sure is scaring those babies," he

asserted when Johnny Littlejohn termed his statement "a phantasm indicative of overactive imagination."

They continued to drive forward in the face of the undersea exodus. When the sheer numbers of fish made headway difficult, Ham, at the controls, adjusted the diving planes and the *Helldiver* knived to a greater depth.

Doc Savage sent the periscope up through its well and scanned the surface.

"Anything?" Monk asked for the third time.

Doc shook his head somberly. "Mostly tuna clippers. One unusual item—a Chinese junk, but we are close enough to the Chinese mainland that junks aren't much of a novelty."

Monk grunted. Leaning against a big pressure gauge, giant Mahli echoed the apish chemist's guttural exclamation. The big bear of a Russian had said little during the trip. Whatever his thoughts were, he kept them to himself.

Seryi had returned to the control room and, conveying her wish with only a touch of the bronze man's arm, indicated her desire to peer through the periscope.

She looked, saw nothing interesting, then indicated a porthole through which various denizens of the deep were flashing past. Even the normally voracious mako sharks were ignoring convenient prey in their haste to flee.

"What on earth could be causing this?" she breathed.

"I wish I knew," the bronze man replied. "I suspected some chemical agent, but the Tokyo Bay samples showed nothing of the kind."

A pleasant notch appeared between the Russian woman's eyes.

"Could it be that this Max Wood has some hideous sea creature under his power—some *thing* so terrible that it frightens even the sharks from the ocean?" she breathed.

Monk, Ham, and Johnny looked at one another. They were thinking of their argument over whether or not a colossal being had lurked down in the Kuril Trench.

Just then the sea turned jet black.

It happened just like that. The seawater outside the *Helldiver* became the color of the ink squirted by a frightened octopus.

The significance of that was not lost on any of them.

"My God!" Ham breathed. "If there *is* such a creature . . ." He didn't finish his thought.

"Doc," Johnny said wonderingly. "Do you remember the legends of the Kraken—a giant devilfish who would ensnare whole ships with its tentacles? It was said he slept for centuries between each attack, and that one day he would wake up for good and bring the world to an end."

"Yeah! That's gotta be it!" Monk howled. "A giant octopus, maybe with poisonous ink. That would explain it!"

"I am afraid of no octopus," Mahli rumbled. "Or any man." The look of unease on his wide features belied his boast. He lapsed back into sullen silence.

"Steady!" Doc said sharply, motioning for silence. He returned to the periscope as Seryi drew closer to him.

Monk, face aghast, had his nose pressed to a porthole.

"If anything like that is out there, we're sure not going to see it in this tar, unless—"

The *Helldiver* gave a violent shake, as if it were a bone grabbed by a very large dog. They were thrown about the inside. Seryi clung to a bulkhead. Mahli clambered to her side to provide support. His eyes shone with affection. Seryi smiled back bravely. The giant was very protective toward his attractive cousin.

A crunching roar assailed their ears.

"It's attacking!" Ham screeched.

Water, in long black yarns, started pouring down from above, indicating ruptured hull plates. The black stuff quickly pooled on the rubber flooring.

"Blow tanks!" Doc rapped urgently. "Surface!"

Monk and Ham tugged control levers. They were bowled to their feet when the sub's nose, made suddenly buoyant, began to rise. Ham had been slow with the stern tanks.

The *Helldiver*'s nose, fitted with a spring-steel bowsprit ram, broke the surface sharply, and poised pointing skyward for an awful moment. Then the sub slapped down, throwing up great sheets of inky brine. It settled, rolling precariously. Finally, the craft righted itself.

They had surfaced near the solitary Chinese junk. It wallowed in a roiling ink-black sea against a distant line of tuna clippers. No other presence—vessel or fish—troubled the open sea.

Monk called that information down from the conning tower. He had been the fastest of the stampede to reach it.

"Did—did we escape it?" Ham wondered aloud.

"We nearly didn't," Doc said grimly as he went up the ladder to Monk's side. "Any closer and that depth bomb would have opened up this boat like a tin can."

"Depth bomb? From where?" Seryi asked incredulously from below.

"That junk yonder is a likely suspect."

That brought everyone up to the tiny conning

tower. It was so cramped they had to take turns at the porthole.

The junk, they saw, was bearing down upon them. It was a sizeable, clumsy-looking craft, being near one hundred tons, and decorated—that was the only word for it—with three sails of pale ribbed cotton.

"Why would a junk try to destroy us?" Johnny asked, not unreasonably.

"Perhaps because we have found Max Wood, *da*?" giant Mahli said fiercely.

The junk was no antique. Swiftly, it warped alongside the *Helldiver,* which was slowly but steadily taking on water, and its crew—it was a distinctly multinational complement—dropped grappling hooks. These snared various points along the sub's razorback spine. The sub was effectively trapped. Submerging was out of the question. And if the *Helldiver* got under way, it might drag the junk along with it, but the submersible would not be able to shake it loose.

Seryi looked at Doc Savage questioningly. His men bore similar expressions. They all had the same question.

Doc said: "We're still taking on water. If it goes on long enough, we'll flood. Then they need only release those grapples and the *Helldiver* will go to the bottom."

"But, Doc," Ham protested, "if they wait that long, wouldn't the sheer weight of our sub drag them down, too?"

"It would," Doc admitted. "But by that time, we'd either be drowned in our compartments, or be forced up on deck, where we would be vulnerable to being picked off by rifle fire."

Monk started to windmill his arms to limber them up.

"I say we charge out there and yank them grapples loose now!"

"I am for that, too," Mahli said, bearing his teeth in a wolfish smile.

Doc Savage shook his head no. "Our only chance," he said, "and it's a slim one, is to surrender."

"Surrender?" Ham bleated. "What about our diving suits?"

"Not enough on board for everyone," Doc said, meeting Seryi's eyes. Seryi nodded bravely. Doc's answering smile was too touched with grimness to be reassuring.

"At least we will have our answers," W. J. Tsumi said without enthusiasm.

That statement ended any further discussion on the matter of resistance.

The complement of the junk was efficient. It kept them all covered with automatic weapons when, led by Doc Savage, the submarine crew emerged from the stunted conning tower. The junk crew, they were interested to see, was composed of Americans, Russians, Chinese, Japanese, and several other nationalities, including the four men from New York who had started the elaborate fish business.

Nate, the straw boss of the latter group—he of the too-shiny carpet-tack eyes—organized a party that lowered stout lines of woven bamboo for them to climb up.

Doc Savage went first. Seryi clasped her arms around his neck and hung on while Doc ascended the line by sheer strength.

After that, the others made their way to the junk's deck. Ham had the most trouble. He tried to climb in such a way that the rough bamboo plaint did not tear his clothes. He fell twice, each time bringing rope burns to his hands and coat front.

Ham succeeded on his third try, assisted by a promise to shoot him dead if he didn't stop clowning around. This promise was made by Nate the straw boss and backed up by a score of rifle muzzles suddenly converging on Ham's forlorn figure.

Once they had been thoroughly searched and relieved of any articles in their clothing—they had wisely left their supermachine pistols and other useful equipment back in the submarine—the straw boss stepped up to Doc Savage and shoved his weather-beaten face into the bronze man's own.

"Welcome to the bad ship *Puffer*," he sneered. "And don't let the cutey-pie name fool you—this won't be no day cruise."

Doc Savage said nothing, as he was frisked for weapons. None were found—which might have had more to do with the wary haste with which the frisking had been conducted than the absence of any weapons. The bronze man towered over his captors.

The others submitted to similar treatment. Then, under the prodding of rifle muzzles, they were escorted below deck to a small cabin.

On the way, Monk pointed to a design affixed to the middle four-cornered sail, a silver fish. It was very round, like a balloon with fins and an unnerving, wide-eyed stare. Its tiny jaw hung down in an expression of open-mouthed terror. "Look familiar?" he asked.

Monk was told to shut up. He growled a surly protest, and was shoved forward for his pains.

The dark innards of the junk smelled bitterly of chemicals. They entered a cabin whose door was pushed open for them. It was slammed shut on the broad back of Mahli, the last to enter. He landed on hands and knees, and picked himself up swearing in voluble Russian.

They saw at once that the cabin was already occupied.

"Doc Savage!" Baker Eastland said, incredulously, jumping up from a rude bunk. "They captured you, too?"

"Obviously," Doc said, bitter-voiced.

Celia Adams was with the ichthyologist, they were unhappy to see. She started right in: "Some rescue party this turned out to be! Mr. high-and-mighty Doc Savage. Humph! I see you didn't do so well for yourself."

"Shut up, Celia!" Baker Eastland yelled. "I've had enough—"

"Don't you talk to me that way!" the blonde noise-maker flared. "Look at what you've got us into. We were supposed to be married by now. What will my father think? And my relatives?"

"Oh, brother," Monk groaned, rolling his tiny eyes.

Baker Eastland turned to Doc Savage. "This is Max Wood's boat. I suppose you know that."

Doc nodded. "He's aboard?"

"Yes. And he's been expecting you. That's why he's kept Celia and myself alive, to use as bait. I thought you all were dead, after what happened back on Plum Island, but—"

Doc cut him off with a chop of one bronze hand. "Suppose you fill us in on the background to this entire affair," he suggested. "We already know something of Wood's plans. It would help if you tell us your role in this."

Baker Eastland sat down heavily. "It's not a pleasant story," he began.

"Then let's get it over with, shall we?"

Baker Eastland ran a hand through his unruly brown hair. His eyes seemed to have lost their lustre, and he had shed noticeable weight.

"You're direct; I'll give you that, Savage. I guess it all started during the war, when I was doing research for the Navy. As you know, there were a lot of crazy schemes dreamed up by the War Department back then to end the war—other than the atom bomb, that is. I guess I was responsible for one of the craziest."

"Let's bob the tail off this critter," Doc interrupted. "I gather this Max Wood will be along any minute."

Eastland nodded. "All right," he said. "I invented a method of driving the fish from a given zone in any ocean. It was originally to be used on the waters around Japan, to starve and demoralize the Japanese people, and bring about eventual surrender. It would have worked, too, except that I hadn't perfected my discovery when Hiroshima and Nagasaki happened. By then, it was too late. I finished the project, but the War Department had no use for it, and I couldn't convince anyone else of its value.

"Well, about a year ago, I was approached by Max Wood, who called himself a scientist, and—well, looking back, I can see he was cultivating me. He seemed to know a lot about me—almost too much. Well, Celia and I were newly engaged. I was running my own laboratory set-up and making little money. Celia didn't want to get married until I had enough to support her the way she was used to. She was going to break the engagement. I—I loved her. I was crazy about her. Well, Max offered me a lot of money for the 'fish frightener,' as I called it. He wouldn't say what he wanted it for, but he knew about it because I had told him the story one night when he and I got tight together. I'm ashamed to say that I gave in."

Baker Eastland sat dejected some moments. He was pale, haggard, unhappy. Celia Adams opened her mouth to say something, but thought better of it.

"After Wood got the secret," he continued, "I had second thoughts. I had a private detective follow him, and found out he was testing it in Quincy Bay. The fishing died out. Then, he tried it way out past Plum Island and succeeded in driving the sea life toward shore. I didn't understand his purpose—he wasn't using it to blackmail anyone, so far as I knew—but I could see what a devastating tool the fish frightener was."

"So you decided to bring the matter to me?"

"Yes. But the private detective I hired turned out to be a crook. Wood bribed him to betray me, then he was killed. I read about this before I could get to you. That tipped me off that I was being followed. I still don't know what Wood plans. We've been here for almost a week. We don't even know where on earth we are."

"In the Sea of Japan," Doc informed him. "Wood is denuding the waters around the Japanese Islands of all sea life."

Eastland's face, if possible, got even more pale.

"Good grief! How big is this thing?"

"*How big is World War Three?*" a cool voice asked from the cabin door.

IX

THE WAR SOWER

The man who entered the junk's cabin leveled a Luger pistol fitted with a "snail" magazine whose thirty-two rounds provided near-submachine gun proficiency. But that was not what gripped Doc, Monk, Ham, and Johnny Littlejohn, holding them momentarily speechless.

The man was, on the surface, not unusual. He was neither short nor tall, heavy nor thin. His hair and his eyes were dark—not brown or black, just dark. His face had a studious quality enhanced by the kind of Tojo-style shell-rimmed glasses that had been popular before the war. It was a serious face, but one seemingly devoid of character because of the very carved-in-wood studiousness of it. One knew at a glance that this was the face of a thinker. But its impassivity of expression betrayed nothing of the content of the thoughts behind it, and ultimately rendered the face a quietly forgettable one.

Ham's voice was a choked cry. "Good Lord!"

"I'll be superamalgamated!" breathed Johnny hoarsely.

"Lemme at 'im!" Monk glowered, starting forward.

The Luger swung in Monk's direction. He might have been shot right then and there but for Doc Savage's quick action. The bronze man blocked the apish chemist with an outflung arm. Monk stayed put, his pig eyes burning.

Doc Savage was a man of nerve; he had been trained for his life's work by renowned scientists and experts in such fields of endeavor as had been deemed useful for the Galahadian life that his father had planned for him. Considerable effort had been expended in inculcating him with the importance of emotional self-control. That control was not manifested in his metallic features now. The bronze man wore the expression of a man who had happened upon his own tombstone.

"Eastland!" Doc hissed urgently. "Is this the man you know as Max Wood?"

Shocked by the vehemence of the bronze man's question, Baker Eastland found his voice. It was a croak: "Yes—yes, it is. *Isn't* it?"

"No," Doc returned tight-voiced. "In the Philippines, we knew him as Jack Thomas. But that is not his true name, either. This man is Jonas Sown. *He died over three years ago.*"

A peculiar and unsettling silence followed, one understood perhaps only by Monk, Ham, and Johnny. They, along with Doc Savage, had encountered Jonas Sown once before, at the end of the war. They had seen him shot down and were convinced of his death. But more than the seeming impossibility of this man's resurrection, there was their knowledge —never proven— of what he had accomplished before his reported death.*

Seryi Mitroff broke the silence. Turning to Doc Savage, she asked: "You make it sound as if this one were the devil himself."

Not taking his flake-gold eyes off the man he called Jonas Sown, Doc said: "He is. Unless circumstances three years ago misled us horribly, this man you see

*The Screaming Man

before us, directly or indirectly, was responsible for the outbreak of the Second World War."

Seryi looked at the slim, scholarly Jonas Sown. Her expression warped several times confusedly. "But I—I have never heard of this man. How could that be?"

"That," Doc said, "is a question I would like answered myself. What about it, Sown—or do you prefer Wood?"

Jonas Sown permitted himself a wry smile. "Because I chose to work behind the scenes, like a master puppeteer." Seeing the bronze man's startled expression, he said to him: "Oh, yes, it is all true. I'm afraid most of the credit for that war is mine. My emotion-controlling device, which I was forced to drop into the sea when I discovered you aboard the *Empress Margaret* shortly after she had sailed from Manila, was indeed the trigger for the outbreak of hostilities in 1939—and for that matter, for certain tests even before then, in Manchuria and Spain."

"Nonsense," Seryi snapped. "This is nonsense. What kind of machine could incite entire nations into war?"

Jonas Sown emitted a short, barking laugh. "Nothing so grandiose as that, I assure you. I worked my will through the emotional states of certain heads of state."

"Another lie!" Seryi flared. "If what you say contained one shred of truth, then Hitler and Stalin would never have fallen out. Or do you claim credit for that event as well?"

Mahli's booming laugh echoed the biting sarcasm of Seryi's question.

"I believe it was Lincoln who said that a house divided against itself cannot stand," Jonas Sown retorted. "The same can be said of an alliance—or a world. The nonaggression pact between Germany and Russia suited my purposes until the low countries fell. Then

I—ah, *incited* Hitler to turn upon Russia. A miscalculation on my part. The Soviet resolve was more steely than I would have imagined."

Mahli's mirth trailed away. Seryi looked stunned. She looked to Doc Savage with questioning eyes.

Doc Savage, held almost spellbound in fascination, asked: "It is true, then, that Adolf Hitler was one of your underlings?"

Sown shrugged, the light reflecting off his coin-shaped glasses so as to make him momentarily appear to be blank-eyed. His machine pistol never wavered from Doc and the others.

"Let us say I had . . . influence over the late *fuehrer*," he said crisply. "I am, or was, it might interest you to know, a neuro-physician. My emotion-controlling machine was the end product of many years—a lifetime, really—of research and experimentation. It worked enormously well, producing hatred, anxiety, fear, and other negative emotions among the leaders and people in Germany, Japan, and elsewhere. Unfortunately, this device was not very flexible in what emotions it inspired. For example, it could not be made to generate positive emotions—not that I had any use for such trifles."

Doc, as much out of scientific curiosity as out of concern that Sown would kill them all once he'd finished boasting—which was clearly what he was doing now—put forth another question: "This device of yours sounded, and still sounds, more than a little far-fetched. How can you expect us to swallow—"

"My device," Jonas Sown said slowly and formally, "was partly the result of my delving into Chinese philosophy. The Chinese, the ancient Chinese at least, espoused some remarkable ideas on the nature of the human mind. A learned scholar whom I believe you knew, Wo To Sei-gei, taught me much, and I applied it well. This junk, for example, is my home and my headquarters, and has been ever since I 'died.'"

"You did not die," Johnny Littlejohn retorted hotly.

"Quite true. I was shot—several times—in the belly. I very nearly died. The Allied authorities preferred to conceal that fact. I was operated on, under an assumed name, in a Manila hospital and later flown back to the United States for rehabilitation. But the San Francisco army hospital in which I had been placed mysteriously caught fire. The body found in my room, needless to say, was not mine. My U.S. agents were responsible for that particular feat of deception."

"Just what is your goal, Sown?" Doc Savage demanded. "You can't be serious about what you said a few minutes ago—that nonsense about World War Three."

Sown's pride was slightly stung, as Doc knew it would be. The scholarly man adjusted his horn-rimmed glasses before he spoke again.

"The contrary," Sown countered. "This brings me back to my last endeavor. My machine worked to perfection, but it was only an instrument of control, and as such, only as good as the pawns I directed. Unfortunately, my pawns were not as strong as they might have been. Had Germany developed the atom bomb first, matters might have perhaps turned out differently. No matter now. As Professor Littlejohn so ably discovered during his period in the Philippines, when the war drew to a close, I left Germany for Japan, then to Japanese-occupied China, and finally to Manila, where we last met. My intention then was to bring my device to America aboard the *Empress Margaret*. My plans at that time need not be detailed here, as I've since abandoned them. But even then I realized that my device was not equal to the lofty goals I had set for myself. I dwelt long on this matter while I convalesced in a place of healing I shall omit to name. It was during those difficult days that I came to understand that I required a weapon capable of wreaking great changes in the world, a weapon potent enough to fell nations, armies, and economies, but one which, unlike the atom bomb, would not produce total destruction.

"Happily, I found such a tool. Spies I had planted in the American War Department told me of a secret that had been in the development stages for use against Japan. I knew this was what I needed and sought out Mr. Baker Eastland, presenting myself as a marine biologist and calling myself Max Wood." Sown smiled tightly. "It was a little jest of mine, Wood being the name the authorities had hospitalized me under. But to continue. Eastland's weapon had been perfected—but you all know something of the nature of that weapon, which Eastland called the fish frightener."

Doc knew the answer to the next question, but asked it anyway: "This fish frightener—how do you propose to trigger another global war with it? Isn't that a hatful of trouble to expect to develop from such a tool, as you call it?"

"Come now, Savage," Jonas Sown said impatiently. "You are a world-renowned genius, perhaps as much an intellectual giant as myself. You learned at the feet of Wo To Sei-gei, as I did. You saw the results of my test in Quincy Bay: the fish gone, the local economy hurt, the authorities, never dreaming it was not a natural phenomenon, completely helpless. At Plum Island, I succeeded in driving all sea life toward land, proving that I could turn the fish frightener to positive use should I need to."

"Why those two localities?" Doc asked.

"Plum Island happened to be one of my network of hiding places," Sown supplied. "As for Quincy, you can thank Miss Adams for that suggestion. In my brief acquaintance with her, I learned to detest everything about the place." Sown gave a perfunctory bow in Celia Adams's direction. "You see, Miss Adams never ceased to speak of it in such relentlessly glowing terms."

Celia Adams colored uncomfortably, but offered no comment.

"And Tokyo?" Doc prodded.

"You have seen for yourself the shambles that Tokyo is becoming," Sown explained. "Soon, all of Japan will have overthrown the American Occupation, inspired by my agents, and Japan will go communist."

"What good would that do you?" Mahli rumbled. "You are not communist."

"No, I am not. But soon this whole area of the world—Russia and all of Asia—will fall under the Iron Curtain. This is already transpiring in China. By that time, I will have built a new emotion-manipulating device and the communist leaders will fall under my power. The Russians are already far along in their aims—which are my aims as well. At the appropriate time, I will merely step in and direct their achievements toward my own ends."

"Which are?" Doc Savage demanded.

Jonas Sown's face took on a look of profound astonishment.

"Why, to control the world," he said, "to rule it. I'm surprised you hadn't figured that out already. I want to do what no one in history has ever succeeded in doing. Alexander the Great, Hannibal, Tamerlane, Genghis Khan, and a very few others, are reputed to have ruled the world at one time or another, but this was not exactly true, of course. They held sway over only the known world as they understood it. I want to dominate the *entire* globe."

"This guy's nuts!" Monk said, but it was almost a question. No one answered it. Jonas Sown, innocuous, yet clearly dominating the rocking cabin by his will as much as by his weapon, had already changed the course of recent history. He could do it again—already had, it seemed.

"Communist Japan will declare war on the United States," Sown continued smoothly. "My network of agents have weapons and planes—you encountered two of them, I believe—cached all over the world. Russia will join Japan. By the time my agents in China have finished their work, China will be an Iron Curtain country, too."

Doc Savage's melodious trilling permeated the creaking cabin. There was nothing pleasant in its note.

"Yes, Savage," Sown offered, "the communist take-over in China is one financed and directed by myself. I did not originate it, of course. I merely, shall we say, *appropriated* it. Doubtless, it would have failed without me."

"It may yet fail," Doc Savage warned. "You seem to be casting your lot with some rather unpredictable elements. The slightest miscalculation and this half of the world could be embroiled in a political conflict with no certain ending. You reckon without the reasoning power of the human brain. No one wants another world war—particularly the Japanese people."

"You are talking about men's hopes, Savage. I will admit that peace is much desired in the world today. But just as all men have brains with which to reason, so too do they possess stomachs which must be fed. This is the Achilles' heel, if you would, of civilization. Men's stomachs. I am striking at Japan through its vast, empty belly. For want of food—in this instance fish—they will do anything I desire. Kill, die, turn on one another. Anything."

"It can't work, Sown," Doc Savage said evenly.

Jonas Sown's thin smile overspread his intelligent-looking features like a bloodless wound.

"You will never know," he said pleasantly, "because now it is time for you to die. Starting with this traitor!" And Sown turned his vicious machine pistol in the direction of W. J. Tsumi.

Doc Savage was not taken by surprise. He had seen the whitening of Jonas Sown's trigger finger moments before he spoke the death sentence. He was tensed and ready.

Doc never completed his desperate and possibly doomed attempt to jump Jonas Sown. He knew the attack would probably result in his death, or severe wounding, but he could give the others a chance to stop the mad neuro-physician. Seryi Mitroff saw Sown's trigger finger pale, too, and sensed the bronze man's intent.

In a blink of an eyelash, several things happened with brain-tricking coincidence.

Doc Savage sprang forward.

Seryi Mitroff tripped him expertly, and moved in on Sown herself.

The machine pistol ripped once, tonguing a long flare of yellow flame—and the cabin became bedlam.

Doc found his feet, slipped on the slick—something wet was suddenly underfoot—floor, and got up again. Monk, Ham, and Johnny swarmed over Jonas Sown, grabbing for his weapon. W. J. Tsumi, his toadlike visage the hue of weathered ivory, struck a cabin wall. He slid down, leaving a red blotch and some of his viscera on the wall. When he opened his mouth to say something, a torrent of blood rushed out. Celia Adams screamed. Somewhere Mahli was roaring rage in gutter Russian. Out in the corridor, men drummed down companionway steps.

"Monk!" Doc yelled. "Knock Sown out; haul him inside before the others come."

"Gotcha!" Monk squeaked.

Turning away, the bronze man raked the room with his eyes. Tsumi sat slumped, unquestioningly dead. Doc found Seryi Mitroff. She was on her side, and there was blood everywhere. It was impossible to tell exactly whose it was. But Doc knew the Russian girl was still alive, because he heard his name whispered, his given name.

"Clark. . . ."

He brushed hair away from her eyes. They were closed. The pulsing of her throat was thready.

Gunfire ripped out again. Doc looked up. Monk and the others had fallen back. Monk had the Luger and was firing it, but Sown was not there. The doorway was full of angry bullets. They gnashed at the frame like blunt teeth.

"Almost had Sown!" Ham said breathlessly. "But his men started firing at us. Sown ran smack into the fusillade. It's a miracle he wasn't chopped to ribbons."

"I'll say this for them," Monk added. "They're a well-trained bunch. They almost nailed us, but gave Sown a wide berth." Monk noticed the crumpled and obviously dead form of W. J. Tsumi and then the bronze man kneeling over Seryi Mitroff. Mahli towered over them, breathing jerkily like a man choking down sobs. "How is she?" Monk asked softly.

Doc looked up at the hairy chemist. "In a bad way. Can we bull our way out of here?"

Monk hefted the Luger. "One gun. Not many shots left. But we'll have to try something. And pronto."

"I'll create a distraction," the bronze man said, his eyes on Seryi's face, which reflected nothing of the pain she must be experiencing, he realized with admiration. It was placid and Madonna-like, as it had been all the time he had known her—a very, very short time, he realized suddenly.

Doc gathered up bedding from the bunk and wadded it in the middle of the floor. He removed a coat button, placed it on the bedding. Next, he tore another button off, this one from his hip trouser pocket. He moistened this with his tongue, told the others to close their eyes, and applied the moistened button to the other.

Doc jumped back, eyes squeezed tightly.

There was an instantaneous chemical reaction. A shower of eye-hurting sparks geysered. The bedding caught fire. Doc tossed the bundle out of the room. The Thermit, he knew, would temporarily blind the gunmen outside. He picked up Seryi Mitroff in both strong bronze arms and, Monk leading the way, dashed for the deck. Seryi lay limp in his arms, her head lolled back.

Mahli positioned himself close to Doc, his face tortured.

"I will use my body to turn any bullets that come toward you both," he said grimly as they fought their way through the smoke-choked companionway.

Doc nodded silently.

The crew had retreated around a corner, where they cursed and tried to blink the burn spots from their optic nerves. They got organized enough to stick their weapons around the corner and snap off a few blind shots. Unfortunately for them, they peered around the corner after that to ascertain if their undisciplined shooting had had any effect. This proved to be their undoing.

Monk shot two of the men—one was the sandy-haired, sunburned one called George—right between the eyes. Doc Savage, worried about Seryi, said nothing about Monk's action, although he personally disapproved of Monk's killing and always had.

Yelling lustily, Monk charged the corner leaping and firing. The noisy combination was demoralizing enough to trigger a general retreat. The Sown gunmen fell back in haste.

"The coast is clear!" Monk howled with glee. "Let's go!"

They banged their way to the companion steps.

The deck was swarming with men, but they were congregated forward of the wheelhouse, busily taking up firing positions. Sown was among them. They couldn't see him, but his voice came to them clearly. He was marshaling his men like a field general.

"The stern!" Doc yelled in Mayan. Mahli, Eastland, and a sobbing, hysterical Celia Adams followed, although they didn't understand the order.

The stern of the junk was a broad, high poop deck, typical of junks. The three batwing sails shielded them from view of the crew, but would not turn bullets once serious firing commenced.

Sown yelled, *"Open fire!"* in half a dozen languages over and over again. The storm of metal began then. Slugs punched through the sails like pencils thrust through paper, and buried themselves in the fine teak rail. They made ugly, voracious sounds chewing into the planking.

The bullets forced Doc and the others to drop to their stomachs on the high afterdeck, but the sound of approaching footsteps told them their moments of relative safety were numbered.

"This gun's empty, Doc," Monk yelled. "We gotta jump—right now!"

Doc, cradling Seryi, nodded harriedly. They all crawled to the back rail while bullets punched the quiltlike cotton sails with spiteful relentlessness. An occasional rib-breaking noise told of a bamboo sail stiffener snapping in two. Under the barrage, the rearmost lugsail was coming apart like a moth plucked by nervous fingers.

"Monk," Doc ordered. "You drop into the water. I'll throw Seryi down to you."

"But, Doc! She's unconscious. You can't swim with her in tow. They'd pick you off in a minute. It would be suicide. For all of us."

"I'll handle her—just catch her, Monk!"

Monk hesitated, his tiny eyes shifting from his leader to the fast-disintegrating sails.

Ham crawled up, his face drained of color. "Monk's right, Doc. We barely have a chance as it is. Leave her—"

"Mahli, I must depend on you," Doc rapped in Russian, but his instructions were never completed, because Monk's hairy red fist suddenly exploded off the point of the bronze man's jaw and dazed him.

It was doubtful that even the powerful Monk could have caught Doc Savage by surprise under any other circumstance. As it was, the burly chemist's blow did not knock the bronze man out. His eyes remained open, but they were dazed and uncertain. Doc was what was commonly called out on his feet, even if he wasn't, technically, standing up.

"I'm sorry, Doc," the apish chemist said, and his face showed it. "Ham, get overboard. I'll toss Doc in; the water should bring him around, but you never know."

"Right."

Ham and the others jumped for their lives, hugged the stern of the boat on either side of the huge ladlelike rudder. That left Monk alone with his dazed leader and the giant Russian, Mahli. The apish chemist lay with his body shielding Doc against the stray wood-gouging bullet.

Monk looked at Mahli. Their faces were but inches apart. Then a live grenade bounced between them.

They saw it in the same instant. Monk reached out for the deadly projectile. Mahli's huge paw closed over it first.

Rearing up, the big Russian flung it back in the direction it had come. He yelled something defiant and inarticulate.

Monk didn't wait to see what happened next. He hefted the bronze man to the rail and pushed him over. Doc made a great splash. Climbing onto the rail, Monk followed.

The detonation illuminated the night as a sudden, violent white flare. The sound was muffled. The sound of the explosion, that is. It was immediately overtaken by an assortment of yells and screams.

More grenades detonated and Mahli dropped off the high poop just ahead of a shower of splintered wood and hot metal fragments.

When Monk surfaced, Doc Savage was once again conscious in the black—it was still the color of octopus ink—water.

Ham and Johnny had to grab the bronze man's arms to keep him from climbing the long stem of the tiller back to the high poop deck.

The look in Doc Savage's agate-hard golden eyes then was one they would never forget.

X

SEA HELL

They watched the bullets hitting the surface with a sick fascination. They fell like intermittent rain, in big, widely spaced drops. The nearest came within two feet of where they bobbed under the overhang of the junk afterdeck and gave them some bad moments. But they soon realized that Jonas Sown's men, gathering up at the junk's stern rail, could not angle their fire acutely enough to reach them.

Jonas Sown soon realized that, too, and the scholarly neuro-physician was screaming some rather unscholarly phrases.

Spitting out inky brine, Mahli said: "They will set boats down, next."

Doc Savage, treading water next to the giant Russian, said nothing, and had said nothing for several minutes. He was expending all of his energy in regaining control over his emotions. His massive chest expanded and contracted with muscular regularity as he strove to get his jerky breathing back to normal. The cords of his throat swelled and pulsed. His golden eyes were whirling, wild. But as he gradually brought himself under control, the tiny winds that played in their aureate depths ceased their violent play.

Ham bobbed into view just as Baker Eastland had

silenced Celia Adams's repeated and nerve-jarring statement that they were all going to die with a hard slap and a harder, "Shut up, Celia!"

Ham said: "I got the air lock open. If we stay calm, we should be able to get aboard the *Helldiver* without them knowing it."

Doc nodded, and Ham started to offer some reassuring words, but knew there was nothing he really could say. The dapper lawyer got the others organized.

One by one, they swam under the junk's flat keel and, in the ink-black water, found their way to the air lock. It was merely an open well in the underside of the submarine, but when they poked their heads up, there was air.

"Doc should be here any moment," Johnny said, gasping. "We'll wait for him."

"Think he'll ever speak to me again?" Monk asked plaintively. No one offered the homely chemist any reassurance.

They climbed up into the craft to await the bronze man.

The submarine had taken on a great deal of water in the forward compartments, which they had sealed off prior to evacuating the crippled submersible. Less than an inch of the black-hued solution covered the rubberized flooring and they took pains not to touch any electrical apparatus as they tried to make themselves comfortable.

At the stern of the junk *Puffer,* Doc Savage treaded water. His sharp ears caught the splash of boats being lowered into the water. He felt in a hidden pocket for the folding grapple and nylon line which he habitually carried. It had escaped discovery when they were searched. With it, he could snag the rail and silently regain the deck. There was a fair chance he could locate and carry Seryi away before they spotted him. He weighed the grapple in his hand, considering his chances.

Seryi was out cold, probably in shock from blood loss. The longer he waited, the more grave her situation was likely to become. Doc knew he could manage the swim to the *Helldiver* with her, but he would have to travel under water to avoid being shot from above. The swim would be no ordeal for the bronze man, who could hold his breath for extended periods of time. But without one of his compact diving lungs for Seryi, she stood an excellent chance of drowning.

Doc Savage wrestled with the problem for many minutes.

Then, without expression on his face, he slipped into the intensely black water.

"Gosh, Doc," Monk said when the bronze man climbed aboard the *Helldiver,* "we thought for a while there you weren't coming."

Doc ignored the homely chemist and sought out Baker Eastland. He found him conversing with Johnny Littlejohn.

"Eastland, is this blackness in the water the result of your fish frightener?" Doc asked, brittle-voiced.

"Why, yes. It's a toxic solution, rather like the Shark Chaser invented during the water. If you recall, Shark Chaser was developed for use by pilots if they went down in water infested with man-eaters. It was a compound which acted on the shark's highly sensitive sense of smell, driving it away. Sharks are ordinarily fearless, but certain natural scents, such as the smell of dead shark, for some reason drive them away like a skunked hound."

"Shark Chaser is largely copper acetate," Doc said, "with enough black dye mixed in to temporarily turn seawater black."

"The dye was for psychological effect," Eastland supplied. "It didn't affect the sharks, but it made a pilot, bobbing in the water while he waited for the rescue plane, feel somehow safer."

"Even an unlimited quantity of copper acetate would not produce the widespread denuding of ocean life we witnessed during our Pacific crossing," Doc pointed out.

"True. My fish frightener is an improvement upon Shark Chaser, not merely a larger application of the same chemicals. As you know, one of the drawbacks of Shark Chaser is that it creates a stationary underwater cloud. A fast-swimming shark can sometimes pass through it unaffected. I'm an ichthyologist, but my specialty is ichthyotoxism—poison fish. It was while experimenting with a new and different kind of shark repellent that I made the breakthrough that led to the fish frightener. I discovered the existence of a Red Sea fish—the frilly flatfish—that secretes a powerful natural milk which sharks find so unappetizing that they will spit the fish out rather than endure it. Because it's an organic toxin, not manufactured, it was a thousandfold times more powerful than copper acetate and not easily diluted in saltwater. The sea is full of creatures possessing such natural defenses against predators—rays, blowfish, scorpionfish, toadfish, stonefish, even some species of shark and catfish. I collected as many as I could, extracted the various toxins, and concocted a kind of witches' brew. It was vile stuff, almost impossible to work with. But I found a way to concentrate it into a dry chemical for easy storage and dispersal. When drawn into the naris, or nostril, it causes virtually all species of fish to succumb to blind, unreasoning panic."

"What is the significance of the puffer?" Doc asked. "Its natural toxins are poison to humans, not inimical to sea life."

"That is some quirk of Wood's—or Jonas Sown as you call him," Eastland explained. "While I've been his prisoner, he has revealed certain things to me. As you know, the puffer when disturbed inflates its body in order to appear larger and more formidable than it is. Sown adopted the inflated puffer as the symbol of his master plan. He has a taste for puffer flesh, too, despite—or maybe because of—the risks involved."

"That explains why he painted its image outside our headquarters," Johnny interjected. "It was the perfect pictorial representation of piscatorial apprehension."

"So the fish frightener works through action on the olfactory receptors of sea life, is that it?" Doc asked.

Eastland nodded. "Mixed with seawater, it creates a solution that stimulates an overpowering fear reaction in all fish and other underwater life, provided they have brains and any type of a nervous system. It turns the water black temporarily because the dry chemical itself is black. But the blackness thins out quickly."

"I tested the waters of Tokyo Bay and found no chemical trace; why is that?"

"After a few days, the solution disperses; the spent toxic material precipitates to the ocean floor and eventually disintegrates," Eastland explained. "There would be no trace, unless perhaps you tested the silt of the seafloor."

Doc nodded. He recalled the floating black specks that swirled along the ocean floor as they had made their trans-Pacific run. It was the most likely of several theories he had come up with to explain the phenomenon. "Then Sown is probably introducing the stuff into the sea through vents in the junk's hull."

"That's my guess," Eastland said. "What are we going to do? We're back where we were an hour or so ago. All they have to do is release this sub and we'll drown."

Doc got the others together and explained the situation to them; not that it needed explaining, but he felt that if he presented their plight to them in this way, they would not be as likely to panic. He did not mention Seryi at all, but her fate was a shadow looming over his mind throughout the tense discussion.

"Sown has to be stopped," Doc concluded. "Here and now. We all know the stakes in this affair and we can't retreat because there may not be another chance for us—or for the world."

"What do you suggest, Doc?" Ham interjected. He twisted his dark sword cane in nervous hands.

"They won't expect us to counterattack immediately, so that is what we will do. Eastland and Miss Adams will stay here, because they are not trained for our type of work."

"No, I'm responsible for all that has happened," Eastland said firmly. "I'm coming."

Doc nodded. "Miss Adams?"

Celia Adams was perched on a fold-down bench. Her frock looked as if it had been smeared with coal dust and then hosed down. Her now-matted blonde hair was streaked with grays and blacks. She started to speak, cleared her throat several times without success.

Celia's blue eyes were downcast, defeated. She did not raise them when she at last spoke.

"I—I'm staying here," she said weakly.

No one was surprised at that.

The tramping of feet on the hull plates over their heads caught their attention. Muffled voices mixed in with the sounds.

"Oh-oh," Ham muttered. "We have callers."

"You ain't woofing," Monk rejoined.

Doc went to the conning tower hatch. It had been dogged tight. Nevertheless, the bronze man took the wheel in both metallic hands. He exerted relentless pressure. The cords in his neck stood out with the strain. The wheel would not turn. Doc's fine white teeth showed and perspiration crawled down his face, creating clear rills of the black streaks already there.

Came a tentative banging topside. Someone was knocking on the opposite side with a tool or possibly the butt of a gun.

Everyone held their breaths, their eyes on Doc Savage.

In Doc's corded hands, the wheel gave a sudden creak. It moved slightly. Doc paused, and redoubled his efforts. They were rewarded by another creak and jerk of the wheel.

The banging continued, picking up volume and violence. Cursing commands to get the hatch undogged reached their ears. It pierced the hull with amazing clarity, considering the *Helldiver's* iceberg-proof design. But the wheel held.

Doc gave a final jerk.

Only then did the bronze man step away from the hatch.

"I daresay," Ham ventured, "that Goliath himself couldn't free that wheel now."

"We have work to do," Doc said grimly.

They got together various equipment they'd need—the tiny supermachine pistols which fired only mercy bullets, much to Mahli's disgust, and the gas and smoke pellets which Doc had used in different forms for many years. Faced with the enormity of the task before them, Doc reflected for the first time on how peculiar and ineffectual his gadgets were. The mercy bullets took time to stupefy their victims, time enough for return shots to be squeezed off. The various gases vaporized too quickly sometimes, or were subject to being blown back in their faces. What if those calamities befell them now? What would happen to the world? Even if they won, even if Jonas Sown were destroyed, what would happen to the world in the coming years, with its atom bombs and Iron Curtains and new would-be political despots?

Doc Savage shook off those pessimistic thoughts as giant Mahli complained boisterously about the puny supermachine pistols. His complaining seemed to be of the loud, habitual kind. His wide face betrayed concentration on the matter at hand and nothing of concern or grief over the question of Seryi's fate. Doc realized then how much like his beautiful cousin Mahli was, and that their shared self-control was probably a consequence of the brutal Russian experiences against the Nazis, and not a family trait. Doc admired that in them both; right now, panic clutched his vitals like steel tongs. He fought the unaccustomed sensation.

With the insistent banging and shouting on the hatch still ringing in their ears, they exited the sub through the air lock. Doc went first, after apprising the others of his plan. It was a simple and direct one; under the press of events it had to be. That did not mean it would work, and the bronze man mentally recited a silent prayer as he cut through the black water.

He surfaced before the men on the sub's spine saw him. He tossed the "scare" grenades, which broke and belched quantities of boiling black smoke. In addition to the smoke, there were chemicals in the smoke that were harmless but smelled exactly like mustard gas. To someone familiar with the smell, it was a disconcerting experience to find oneself in the midst of it, utterly unable to see.

Several of the junk crewmen were crouched over the stubborn hatch. They were using a hammer and cold chisel on the wheel spokes. One spoke and a portion of the wheel's thick rim had been broken off, a testament to the bronze man's Herculean strength.

Others stood guard, but their eyes were on the hatch as well.

The sepia smoke rolled toward them.

"Gas!" one howled. It was the straw boss, Nate.

The speed at which the men at the hatch abandoned their efforts was almost comical. They stumbled into one another. Rifles, jarred, fired into the air. The pall enveloped them, and simple panic turned to pandemonium.

Like fleas raked by a fine-toothed comb, the men jumped off the sub and into the water.

Monk and the others had stationed themselves on either side of the sub's flanks. They overpowered the crewmen with fists and clubbed weapons. A few eluded these inducements to oblivion and tried to strike out for the junk. The spiteful snap of mercy pistols, latched onto single-shot operation, put a stop to that notion.

Dragging their prisoners, Doc and his party clambered onto the *Helldiver*, using its sledlike runners for purchase. Not all of the junk's crew could be brought back aboard, but no one, not even Doc Savage, gave much thought to those who slipped into the India-ink water, still unconscious.

Doc went among the prisoners with a hypodermic needle, injecting them by feel with a stupefying drug designed to keep a foe out of mischief for several hours. Doc attended to the one called Nate last, after extracting from him an estimate of the junk's total manpower. Struggling, Nate blubbered that he was afraid of needles. Monk had to hold him down while Doc administered the drug.

"Hah! Some tough guy he turned out to be," Monk snorted. Sensing that Doc was no longer there, the apish chemist peered through the rolling murk.

The acrid smoke, like a giant from the deep,

ingested the wallowing junk from its prominent bow to its plump stern.

By this time, Doc had snagged the junk's railing with his tiny grappling hook. To his surprise, it caught on the first blind throw. He fervently hoped that was an omen. He went up the line with monkeylike agility. The others followed, using the loops and knots in the cord as handholds.

Doc disposed of two crewmen he encountered in the dark simply by hoisting them over the side. One hit the water, but the other slammed onto the *Helldiver*'s railed hull. He groaned once, then began sobbing uncontrollably.

"We're all here," Monk breathed, dropping from the rail. He shook blackened water off his long hairy arms.

"Bunch up and cut loose with your mercy pistols," Doc said quietly.

They arranged themselves in a tight string across the bow and set the weapons to shuttling and smoking. The sounds the pistols made were like a bullfiddle chorus, discordant and loud.

Yelling in half a dozen languages came back to their ears. Men trampled the deck, all of them heading toward the stern, or possibly below.

"We use other gas now?" Mahli asked fiercely.

"No," Doc warned. "The breeze is blowing back to us; it would do no good." He didn't mention the danger, quite real, that some of the thrown pellets might not break upon impact, and would thus be dangerous to have underfoot when they advanced.

The machine pistols moaned once more. Their surprisingly subdued muzzle-flame barely cut the slowly thinning smoke. The mercy bullets made practically no sound upon impact—only a faint tinkling as the hollow shells dashed themselves against hard surfaces, splashing their volatile anæsthetic. Under the circumstances, it was impossible to know if they were achieving any results.

The deck gave back silence.

"I think we have them cowed," Ham ventured optimistically.

"Perhaps," Doc whispered. "Everyone get down, and we will let the wind carry this smoke away."

They hugged the rolling deck. The smoke stung their eyes a little, made them smart and tear, but it was only a mild side effect of the chemical, one which Doc hadn't been able to remove from the mixture.

Mahli was the first to make out the stern, as much of it as could be examined through the ragged batwing sails.

"The deck would seem to be deserted," he absentmindedly remarked in Russian.

It was. Not a shadow moved, or seemed to move. They had some trouble adjusting their eyes to the lack of light because dusk had so quickly fallen. In the murk, the absence of the smoke was not readily perceptible.

"We got 'em trapped!" Monk howled. "They're either laying for us below or holed up in the wheelhouse."

Doc Savage, eyes on the high poop, saw the spot from which they had jumped what seemed like an eternity ago. There was no sign of Seryi Mitroff anywhere.

He discerned a patch of shadow there, though— which might have been shadow, or perhaps a very large stain on the deck.

Whatever it was, the sight of it sent a cold trickle slithering down the bronze man's spine.

XI

STALEMATE

The sound of Jonas Sown's voice calling his name cut through the bronze man like a knife.

"Savage!" Sown called again. "Do you hear me?"

Doc started to answer, couldn't find his voice, and had to clear his throat noisily. "I hear you," he called back.

"We seem to be at an impasse," Sown yelled back, and his tone sounded odd, probably because he was a man not used to having to raise his voice. The studious ones are almost always that way, and that fact made the bronze man wonder if the bottling-up of his emotions had started Jonas Sown—if that was his real name, for no one knew—on the strange road that had spurred him to cause one world war and then attempt to ignite another in order to fulfill some grandiose dream. Even now, Doc had some difficulty linking the horrors of the past ten years with the serious-faced, bespectacled man whose voice carried over the empty deck. He knew that Jonas Sown was an evil genius unlike any the world had ever before seen, but it baffled the imagination to link the annexation of Austria, the invasion of Czechoslovakia, the Battle of Stalingrad, Midway, and Hiroshima with this one individual. True, Jonas Sown had not directly caused each and every one of those occurrences, but like the man who tips the first domino tile in the chain, it was he who had caused the remainder to topple, even though his fingerprints were not on them all.

"We can't remain in stalemate forever," Sown was saying in an edgy tone.

"He's right, Doc," Monk ventured cautiously, not certain that the bronze man would even acknowledge his existence. Monk's homely face wore expectation like a clown's face; he almost worshiped Doc Savage. What he had done when Doc had hesitated over escaping the junk was unplanned, but necessary. He wasn't convinced that the bronze man was ready to see it that way.

"What do you think we should do?" Monk asked. He looked to the bronze man with expectant puppy-dog eyes.

When Doc said nothing for several minutes, Monk went off by himself and made silent shapes with his fists. For a time the only sound was the dry rustling of the batlike junk sails and the thin voice of Jonas Sown.

Drawing up beside him, Johnny Littlejohn told Monk: "Women always bring trouble." But that did not cheer up the homely chemist.

Jonas Sown was saying: "Savage, the longer we protract this standoff, the more the fish frightener continues to empty into the ocean. You know that, don't you?" Sown, for the first time, sounded truly afraid. But then, his fear of the bronze man had caused him to tip his hand back at the beginning of the affair, when he had sent his men to New York to perform the zany business over the frightened silver fish. The inflated-puffer emblem on the junk sail, Doc reflected, must be a good-luck charm or recognition sign between members of Sown's far-flung group of political agitators. The smartest thinkers are often prone to such idiosyncracies. And even the most powerful of men—and Jonas Sown seemed to be another Napoleon or Hitler—were subject to fright. Jonas Sown felt fear now—fear of Doc Savage.

"We can make a deal, *Ren Beh Chingtung*," Sown yelled, using the Chinese words for Man of Bronze. "Let my men and myself go free, and you may have the junk and the fish frightener. Just allow us to swim to one of the fishing boats nearby and the junk is yours. I know you're a man of your word. What about it?"

The afraidness in the man's voice was a tonic to the bronze man's nerves; he felt his confidence return. A long-ago memory from his youth came back to him; a phrase one of the scores of tutors who had trained him for his strange life—trained him at the behest of this father, who had suffered a strange, unknown misfortune that impelled him to place his only son in the hands of scientists and thinkers—burned clear in his mind. It was a Chinese phrase, Confucian, he recalled, which was imparted to him by Wo To Sei-gei, the same Chinese scholar whom Jonas Sown knew. It was: "True gold fears no fire." It was only a phrase, true, but it inspired confidence then as it did now.

Doc Savage put his concerns out of his mind.

"Before we make any deals," Doc yelled toward the wheelhouse, "you'll have to show your good faith."

"How?"

"Release Seryi Mitroff. No deals until she has been freed."

There was a long, long silence in which the sails rustled. A low moon shone through them, the battens resembling ribs in a mummy's chest.

Finally, Jonas Sown yelled, "All right, the girl is yours." His voice squeaked like a bat's.

The gunfire started in the next breath.

* * *

It was a short burst—a mercy pistol, but it came from the wheelhouse. Wildly, Doc looked toward his own men crouched nearby. One was missing.

"Damn it!" Ham yelled. "Mahli isn't here! He must have snuck off while we were listening to that devil, Sown!"

More guns ripped. There was only one choice now—no choice at all.

"Come on," Doc called, and they charged aft.

The mercy pistol stopped abruptly, and there was a roar of rage, like a wounded bull—obviously Mahli. Glass shattered, wood splintered somewhere. More guns banged. A man flew out of the wheelhouse, obviously not of his own volition. Whooping, Monk clubbed him unconscious.

Other men poured out. They met Doc, Monk, Ham, and Johnny like waves crashing together. After that no guns sounded and there was just the crack of fists on jaws and the grunting of men engaged in very physical work.

Once, a knife flashed for Monk's face and Doc Savage broke the wielder's arm deliberately. Monk looked relieved, and fell on a skulking Japanese crewman with newfound enthusiasm.

"I don't see Sown," Ham Brooks yelled above the melee. He had his sword cane unsheathed—it had been left in the *Helldiver* originally and lately recovered—and was slashing viciously at anyone who came near. He was clearly worked up; ordinarily, he would lightly stab an opponent and let the chemical on the blade's tip do its incapacitating work. Now he was inflicting damage. Strings of blood poured from open cuts all around him.

Doc found Mahli. The giant—his name meant "small" in Russian—had two men in a bear hug and was concentrating on crushing their rib cages like a Madison

Square Garden wrestler. The men were screaming horribly, over and over again. Their faces were red and going purple. They bit their lips in agony, producing foamy blood.

"Mahli, stop!" Doc urged.

The giant only closed his eyes with renewed effort.

"*Cron*, Mahli!" Doc shouted, repeating the command in the Russian's own tongue. "*Cron!*"

When he realized the giant Russian wasn't going to listen to reason, Doc changed tactics.

"Sown!" Doc yelled at the enraged Russian. "Where is he?"

Mahli still did not hear the bronze man—or so it seemed.

"Your cousin, Seryi. Mahli, where is she?"

Mahli gave a last groaning heave and the two men went limp in his great arms, dead. He dropped them without ceremony. Wild-eyed, he looked about for more enemies and latched onto another hapless crewman, after first relieving him of a wicked marlin spike.

Doc let him be. He was in a killing rage, and not too particular about his choice of victims. The bronze man thought he knew why, and the knowledge was a coldness in his marrow.

He went in search of his own answers.

XII

PLENTY

Except for a few strays whom his men chased the length of the junk, the fighting had just about subsided when Doc Savage found Seryi Mitroff's body in one corner of the wheelhouse.

In his heart the bronze man was not surprised. He was surgeon enough to have realized her wounds must have been fatal ones from the start, but he had shoved that knowledge into the darkest corner of his mind and kept it there throughout the last several hours because he did not want to admit the truth, even to himself. It had been important to him that grief not wash over him and cripple his ability to fight Jonas Sown. Too much had been at stake. He had understood that much without letting the terrible realization march through his mind, but it had guided his actions nonetheless. It was the reason why Doc had not reboarded the junk the first time, although he had stood a fair chance of reconnoitering the vessel undetected.

Stone-faced, Doc knelt over Seryi Mitroff's inert form and felt for a pulse. None. Seryi lay on her side, her chest wetly red, and her eyes closed. Doc was grateful that her eyes were closed. It meant she had died without prolonged agony—even if she had died alone and among enemies.

Her oval face was still calm and composed and strong, just as it had been in life. It was the face of a Madonna, classic and in its way, deathless.

Doc became aware of Mahli hovering over him, calm and in control of himself once more. He had not heard him approach. The giant Russian said nothing. He was just there, like silent grief given human form.

The others filed in presently, but they said nothing when they found the bronze man still kneeling over the body.

Up on the deck, feet whetted wood frantically and there was a splash of a sound coming through the seasoned cedar hull.

Johnny Littlejohn dashed up the companionway, and just as quickly plunged down again, stumbling like a daddy longlegs spider.

"Sown!" he yelled breathlessly. "He went overboard!"

Doc Savage, his face warped in flat planes of grief and anger, charged for the door, beating Mahli to the deck.

The sound of splashing brought him to the port rail. The bronze man paused only long enough to get a fix on the swimmer.

Then he stepped onto the rail and followed Jonas Sown into the water.

Sown, a black shape in the black water, struck out for the cluster of nearby tuna clippers. He turned his head only once, at the sound of Doc Savage hitting the water, and frantically redoubled his efforts.

On deck, Mahli picked up a gun someone had dropped. It was not a mercy pistol. The moon was still low, but there was enough light to make out the figures of Jonas Sown and Doc Savage stroking toward the clippers.

"Doc's gaining on him," Monk said excitedly.

Mahli grunted. "The bronze one is fast," he rumbled, "but I have something more fast, *nyet?*" Mahli lay the barrel of his captured pistol across a leveled forearm. He fired once.

Sown twisted in the water. He grabbed for his right knee.

"Good shooting!" Ham breathed. "You got him in the leg."

Mahli fired again, this time hitting Sown's other leg.

Another bullet followed it.

Like a worm impaled on a pin, the neuro-physician floundered in the water as Doc Savage, his arms propelling him in a powerful breaststroke, closed in like a human torpedo.

Attracted by the noise and commotion, the clippers edged in closer.

"This is good sport, *nyet?*" Mahli said fiercely.

None of the others stopped the Russian as he calmly, methodically, and cold-bloodedly emptied the gun into Jonas Sown's thrashing legs.

Mahli kept firing even after the bullets ran out. Then he went in search of another pistol.

In the water, Doc swam to within a handful of yards of Jonas Sown. They could see milky moonlight shimmer off Sown's glasses, which had somehow managed to stay on his face. The reflected light gave the floundering neuro-physician the aspect of a blind insect struggling to keep afloat on a pond.

Ham Brooks used the twin reflections to home in on Sown with a searchlight he found on the wheelhouse roof. He illuminated that patch of water just in time to capture the climax of the chase.

Jonas Sown floated on his back, his incredulous face bobbing close to the surface. Yarns of blood radiated all around him like spreading fingers.

Doc Savage, trailing a wake of disturbed water,

reached out to snare his quarry. He was too late by a foot.

Jonas Sown simply sank.

Arching like a porpoise, Doc Savage followed him down.

The red-tinged black water shook and regathered itself at the spot where they had disappeared.

"Doc'll get him," Monk predicted.

"Let us hope," Johnny said fervently.

Two minutes passed, then three. Ham worked the searchlight, trying to locate any disturbance on the choppy seas. Monk almost dove in. Mahli stopped him with a taunting remark.

"Have you so little faith in your leader?"

Monk subsided. He squeezed the rail hard enough to draw blood.

Moments later, a flurry of bursting air bubbles erupted with a ghoulish gurgle.

Then the bronze man broke the surface. He treaded water momentarily, pushing himself around in place with his arms. In no direction did they spy another swimmer. The searchlight halo made that plain to all.

Finally, Doc swam back to the junk alone.

Doc Savage boarded the junk by climbing up his grappling hook and line, which still trailed down to the water.

"Sown got tangled in one of the clipper nets," Doc informed the others stiffly. "He drowned before I could reach him."

"You were a fool to try to save him," Mahli sneered.

"I had no intention of rescuing Jonas Sown," Doc told him flatly.

Hours later, they had inventoried the casualties. Most of the junk's crew, including the remnants of the New York gang, were either dead or incapacitated.

Monk, Johnny, and Mahli had pumped out the *Helldiver*. After repairs, she would be seaworthy enough for the voyage home, provided they nursed her through the crossing.

Ham had been in touch with SCAP headquarters in the *Dai-Ichi* Building in Tokyo by radio, explaining the situation. U.S. warships were dispatched from different Japanese ports to take charge of the junk and its surviving crewmen. Ham joined Johnny and Monk, who were poking about the junk's innards, to report the news.

"Here's the fish discourager," Monk announced, pointing to several rows of simple devices on the order of oversized hourglasses set into the keel. The top halves of these were filled to capacity with a gritty black material like crushed coal. The bottom halves were empty. Valves in the narrow neck of each hourglass kept the black grit in the upper portions of the glass until a releasing switch was activated. One row of devices was empty, top and bottom. They could see the grilled bases that allowed the stuff to precipitate below.

"I'm not very impressed," Ham sniffed.

"The stuff is just a dry chemical, like Eastland said," Monk explained. "These glass things store it and a timer releases the stuff down into the lower bells, and then into the water through vents in the hull. Not particularly complicated. I've shut 'em all off."

"I've been in touch with Tokyo," Ham said. "Things are still pretty bad there, but I promised them we could turn the situation around. Am I a liar?"

Johnny Littlejohn answered that: "I was just speaking with Eastland. The toxin has to be replenished every six days to keep sea life from a given area. That means it should be wearing off on the other side of Japan. We stopped it here soon enough so that not too much damage was caused. Once the Occupation explains this to the Japanese people, and they are given enough fish to tide them over, everything should be back to normal within a week or so."

"Say, where *is* Eastland?" Monk inquired. "I haven't seen him around the last couple of hours, although that she-foghorn, Celia Adams, has been all over this tub looking for him."

"I think he's trying to avoid her," Johnny said.

From above, they could hear Celia's high-pitched voice. A lower, but angrier, voice joined in—Baker Eastland's.

"Looks like she found him," Ham offered.

They listened, made out no words, but were surprised to hear Eastland's voice more often than the girl's. Then the arguing ceased.

"Sounds like he came out on top," Monk opined.

The ichthyologist came below deck presently to join them.

"I think you're learning to handle your bride-to-be," Monk told him airily.

"You mean my fiancé-that-was," Eastland retorted. "I just broke the engagement."

"Too bad."

"She'll get over it."

Johnny approached the grim scientist. "Eastland, whatever your true intentions, you are responsible for much of what has happened. Have you thought about atoning for your mistakes?"

Baker Eastland looked about the hold and its fantastic profusion of glass devices. "I have," he said. "My fish frightener is a terrible weapon, but in the right hands it could be a boon to all of mankind. Someone who knows what he's doing can use it to herd food fish from the deep, unfished waters of the world and into the coastal fishing grounds where they would do the most good. It could mean plenty for the starving people of the world."

"You'd like to turn your discovery over to Doc Savage, is that correct?" Johnny prompted.

"Yes," Baker Eastland said firmly.

"I'll go tell Doc," Monk said hastily.

Monk Mayfair found the bronze man on the high afterdeck alone. He was leaning on the rail and looking out to sea. Moonlight burnished his metallic skin. His opaque golden eyes resembled frosted glass.

Monk cleared his throat. "Eastland wants to turn the fish gadget over to you."

Doc's nod was almost imperceptible.

Monk looked at the bronze man's back, shuffled his big feet awkwardly.

"Doc?"

"Yes, Monk?" The voice was remote.

"Did I do the right thing? Back when we had to leave the junk, I mean."

The bronze man was silent for a time, during which Monk Mayfair did not breathe.

"Yes, Monk, you did the right thing."

The homely chemist let out a long sigh of relief, but he did not smile. It was not a time of rejoicing, not for Doc Savage.

"You really liked her, didn't you?" he asked after a pause.

When the bronze man didn't reply, Monk left him to his thoughts.

AFTERWORD

To readers of the Doc Savage series, the byline Kenneth Robeson is a magical name, conjuring up images of a strapping two-fisted author with a twinkle in his eye, equally at home in the cockpit of a schooner as he was flying a plane.

In actuality, there was never any such person as Kenneth Robeson. The byline is a fiction the publishing world calls a "house name"—that is, a pseudonym owned by a publishing house, and designed to conceal a multiplicity of writers. House names are most often employed on long-running series as a kind of insurance in case the man behind the byline becomes ill, moves on, or asks for too large a raise. This way the writer may be replaced without the readers becoming upset.

The mythical Kenneth Robeson was first created in 1933 to mask the true identity of the author behind the Doc Savage pulp magazine series, who was, of course, the legendary Lester Dent.

Dent was only 28 in December, 1932 when he sat down to write that first Doc novel, *The Man of Bronze*—reportedly in ten days flat. He had been a professional writer for a difficult three and a half years since the day in June, 1929, when he made his first sale, *Pirate Cay*, to Street & Smith's *Top-Notch Magazine*.

At that time, Dent had been a telegraph operator for the Associated Press, working out of the *Tulsa World* Building. It was the latest of a long line of professions pursued by a restless and energetic Missourian, who had worked oil fields, sold shirts, briefly studied law but had yet to find his place in the world.

When Street & Smith took his first story, Dent, who had grown up reading *Argosy* and other pulp magazines of the day, had visions of freelancing. It took him six months to sell his next story. Then he sold three in a row—all to Street & Smith, one of the most prestigious of the pulp houses.

This brief period of promise was soon dashed. The stock market had crashed. Publishers were tightening their belts or going out of business altogether. Dent plugged on, making the occasional sale, but found it tough going.

"This writing business is an etheric racket," Dent once lamented, "especially when you are on the outside. Nothing is quite as sickening as getting story after story back and wondering 'why?' It takes things out of you. It sort of curls you up. There is nothing concrete to grasp and go to work against. You cannot stand back and look at your completed work as a carpenter can examine the house he is constructing, strangely enough. And when one editor says the figurative roof of your story is too flat, and the next says it is not flat enough, you begin to think yourself dizzy."

Late in 1930, a chance submission to Richard Martinsen's *Sky Riders* magazine brought a telegram suggesting that Dent come to New York City and help fill the pages of his string of magazines with rollicking action stories. With his loyal wife Norma in tow, Dent packed up, drove east, and buckled down to being a pulp writer, filling the pages of *Sky Riders* and *Scotland*

Yard, with the occasional foray into writing radio drama for the *Scotland Yard* radio show.

That was in January, 1931. Both magazines and the radio show were out of business by the spring and Dent found himself in New York without work. The Great Depression had settled over the nation.

Dent floundered around for much of 1931 and the following year, making few sales. Getting back on his writing feet, he began specializing in Western stories. He had grown up on ranches throughout Oklahoma and Wyoming and knew the cowboy life. Occasionally, when a magazine would run two of his stories in one issue, a house name would be affixed to the second story. Dent disliked it when this policy was invoked, but the use of house pseudonyms was standard practice and there was nothing he could do about it.

Dent was very busy writing in February of 1932 when he received a surprise invitation from Street & Smith, with whom he had had no dealings in almost two years. They had begun publishing *The Shadow,* a magazine featuring the exploits of the mysterious radio crime fighter which were written by Walter B. Gibson, writing under the house name of Maxwell Grant.

The offer was to write a Shadow novel. Dent took Street & Smith up on it, and *The Golden Vulture* resulted. But no further Shadow novels were offered to him. In fact, *The Golden Vulture* was to lie unpublished until 1938, when Gibson revised it for publication—the only collaboration between those two pulp titans. The Street & Smith editors were not looking for a replacement for Walter B. Gibson, but for a writer to bring to life a new character who was planned as a high adventure counterpart to The Shadow—Doc Savage.

For a writer who had been experiencing his share of rejects and disappointments—magazines often went out of business before Dent could deliver a story writ-

ten to specific requirements—the opportunity to write
a monthly series like Doc Savage was both a gold mine
and the ultimate job security. Dent leapt into the task
with the same gusto that would later carry him through
his Caribbean treasure hunting adventures and his
light-plane flying phase.

As soon as Dent finished writing *The Man of
Bronze,* he batted out a short story to help *Doc Savage*
editor John L. Nanovic fill out the new magazine's back
pages. To this story, he appended the improbable pseudonym, "Heck Sailing," because he assumed that the
lead Doc novel would carry his personal byline.

Instead, *The Man of Bronze* bore the unfamiliar
name of—Kenneth Roberts.

It's a little-known morsel of Doc Savage trivia that
Street & Smith had christened their new contract writer with the Anglo-Saxon name of Kenneth Roberts.
How they arrived at this particular construction is open
to speculation. Since one of Doc's aides was named
Long Tom Roberts, it's possible that they wished to
create the impression that the stories were being related by a close relative to one of Doc's band of men, just
as they went to great lengths to tout the fictitious
Maxwell Grant as a real person who had been given
access to The Shadow's secret archives for the purpose
of fictionalizing his exploits.

Another interesting possibility was that, consciously
or not, they purloined the name from the Shadow radio
program, whose announcer was Ken Roberts. It was the
practice in those days for the announcer to identify
himself at the end of every broadcast, so Roberts's name
was publicly known.

Whatever the case, no sooner had the first issue of
Doc Savage magazine debuted than the Street & Smith
editors received an angry note from a well-known his-

torical novelist and contributor to the *Saturday Evening Post*, whose name happened to be—Kenneth Roberts.

A hasty meeting was convened, the real Kenneth Roberts was placated, and a new byline was quickly concocted.

Thus was "Kenneth Robeson" born.

Whether it was Roberts or Robeson made no difference to Lester Dent, who complained to an editor in later years:

"I don't see where the house name tradition makes ten cents. And writers will. work more happily when their brain babies come out with their own names on them. My own name on the stuff would have prestige value to me, and wouldn't cost the firm."

As it would turn out, the Robeson name proved to be both a curse and a boon to Dent. A curse because it denied him public credit for his work, and a boon because it enabled others to assume the byline when Dent needed a break from Doc Savage. Which would often happen.

Dent banged out an amazing 15 Docs in his first year on the series. The magazine was an instant hit, selling close to 250,000 copies a month even as, all over Manhattan, entire publishing firms were going out of business. Offers to adapt the character for the burgeoning radio industry began pouring in.

In December, 1933, the Knox Company of St. Louis contacted Street & Smith about securing radio rights to The Shadow, which had gone off the air because parents complained lead character's sinister persona gave their children nightmares. But the show had since been picked up by NBC, so Knox was offered Doc instead. Street & Smith stipulated that Kenneth Robeson would write the scripts. Dent had wisely retained radio rights to Doc.

Knox then made arrangements with the Don Lee

Network, which was headquartered at Station KHJ in Los Angeles, to package the series. *Doc Savage* began airing in February, 1934 at nine P.M. on Sunday nights. Twenty-six 15-minute episodes were broadcast, and in the fall the show was syndicated nationwide and in Canada.

Today, the *Doc Savage* program is so obscure that the identities of its cast are completely unknown. All that survives are carbons of Dent's scripts, which, amazingly, were original episodes and not adaptations of Dent's print stories.

It was the pressure of this radio work that impelled Lester Dent to hire his first Doc Savage ghost writer. It is a time-honored practice for prolific writers of such series to bring in apprentices to help meet deadlines. In this case, Dent turned to an old crony from his Tulsa days, fellow telegrapher Harold A. Davis.

A Colorado native who shared Lester Dent's midwestern roots, Davis had come to New York City from the *Tulsa World* in 1932 to work on the *New York News American*. Davis aspired to write fiction and Dent gave him his first break ghosting the sixteenth Doc novel, *The King Maker*.

Although Dent found that he had to virtually rewrite Davis's draft, Davis went on earning extra money writing short stories for the back pages of *Doc Savage* and companion magazines. As Davis improved, Dent provided him other Doc Savage opportunities. Gradually, he became proficient enough to write Doc novels without supervision, and later went on to become perhaps Dent's most creative ghost writer.

Davis was by all accounts a rather bland person with the reporter's discipline for meeting deadlines. Letters from Davis to Dent indicate his chief motivation in writing Doc was to keep the wolf from his door. He was a redhead who affected a banker's green eyeshade, and about as far from the boisterous personality of Lester Dent as might be imagined.

While Davis ultimately went on to write some twelve Docs, his difficulties with *The King Maker* left Dent without a reliable ghost. Dent simply stopped writing for other magazines and buckled down to the monthly Docs routine and turning out five radio scripts a month.

The *Doc Savage* radio program was not renewed for a second season, in part because Knox used it to peddle a patent medicine called Cystex. Patent medicines were abruptly banned from radio advertising in 1934 by the FCC. Dent, relieved of that writing chore, was nevertheless eager to cut back on his Doc novel schedule and began casting about for new ghost writers.

At that time, pulp writers in New York had formed a group, the American Fiction Guild, which met every Friday at a Manhattan eatery called Rossoff's. There, Dent met many candidates for the job of apprentice Kenneth Robeson.

One was Richard B. Sale, a bespectacled young writer later to go on to fame as a film and television writer. In 1934, he was just getting his feet wet in pulp fiction and was eager to ghost Doc Savage. Sale wrote two sample chapters for *The Mystic Mullah*, from a Dent pilot. Unfortunately, Dent's criticisms were apparently so discouraging to the young writer, he dropped the project. Dent wrote *The Mystic Mullah* himself.

A second American Fiction Guild member who expressed interest was W. Ryerson Johnson, an easygoing contributor to *Adventure, Argosy,* Street & Smith's *Western Story Magazine* and other prestige pulps. He and Dent hit it off and Johnson, who had gotten into the pulp field with the hope of writing science fiction, but got sidetracked into Westerns because that was where the money was, agreed to ghost *Land of Always-Night*.

Although Dent had to polish the book, *Land of Always-Night* proved to become one of the most popular Doc Savage novels ever. Johnson then did *The Fantastic Island*. After that, came *The Motion Menace*.

The Motion Menace may have the most checkered history of any Doc novel. The outline was approved in 1935, but Johnson's draft went astray and Dent shelved the plot for a solid year. Dent ultimately rewrote the book from scratch. It would normally have been published in 1937, but because it involved the destruction of a passenger Zeppelin, which was considered too sensitive a subject in the wake of the *Hindenburg* disaster, it was not printed until 1938—three years after work on it first began.

"On *The Motion Menace*," Johnson recalled, "it was my original idea, and I gave it a softsell in the opening, starting with a house fly buzzing across Doc Savage's desk, and stopping in midair and dropping straight down in front of Doc's face. Doc wonders idly. Next sequence has a seagull seen by Doc from his moving car. Seagull, hitting the invisible motion barrier, drops straight down. Doc's car is the next thing to contact the invisible force. . . .

"Les was more than a little scornful about starting out a Doc Savage novel with just a single fly, and he ended up restructuring the whole story, 'Who do you think you're writing for, *Harper's*? You want to know my audience?' He then told me about a 'scroungy looking pimpleface little kid about ten years old' he had seen on the subway reading a *Doc Savage* magazine. 'Write for him,' Les said."

Johnson, although he remained friends with Dent for many years after, declined any subsequent jobs ghosting Doc Savage.

"Ghosting is a dead alley for a writer," he once said. "It's hunger writing. I never did any more of it than I had to when I needed quick money."

Dent turned next to Martin Baker, who was one of his many secretaries during the period when Dent dictated substantial numbers of his Docs. Baker began work on a Doc entitled "Death's Domain," but soon discovered he hadn't the temperament for writing fiction. Dent completed the story himself, calling it *The South Pole Terror*. Martin Baker's contribution to the finished product—if any—is so negligible as to disqualify Baker from admission to the honored company of Kenneth Robesons.

Early in 1935, when Dent was working with Ryerson Johnson and giving Harold Davis a second shot at Doc, John L. Nanovic hired another Kenneth Robeson.

It had been Street & Smith's hope to bring out *Doc Savage* every two weeks, just as with *The Shadow*. Dent had no interest in being a two-novel-a-month pulp writer, and made no bones about this.

And so entered Laurence Donovan. Very little is known about Donovan. He seems to have begun writing in the late 1920s, and gravitated to writing back-of-the-book stories in *Doc Savage* and *The Shadow*. Nanovic decided to try him on a Doc novel. His first effort, *Cold Death*, proved so successful a replication of the Dent style that Donovan went on to write a total of nine Docs.

Donovan's Docs are actually a rough-hewn group, lacking Dent's whimsical humor and smoothness of style. But readers of the day failed to detect the darker, more violent tone, which the editors had asked Donovan to employ as a contrast to Dent's often tongue-in-cheek approach.

The plan to double Doc Savage production died when the Street & Smith road men discovered that *Doc*

Savage Magazine enjoyed a steady sale throughout each month, unlike *The Shadow* which sold out quickly, leaving the newsstands bare of copies, and readers hungering for more. It made more sense to increase the print run and exploit the full thirty-day sales period. Doc Savage fans today experience mixed emotions when they think of the novels that were never written—just as they breathe a sigh of relief that there aren't another eighty or ninety expensive issues to collect!

After penning *He Could Stop the World* in December, 1935, Donovan was given the opportunity to write a new series, *The Skipper*, about a hard-bitten seagoing Doc Savage clone named Cap Fury. He added a Shadow imitation, *The Whisperer*, to his chores soon after. Neither magazine survived the 1937 recession, and shortly after that Donovan fell out of John Nanovic's good graces—reportedly due to erratic behavior. He went on to ghost other long-running series characters for rival publishers, and his byline ceased to appear after the war.

The inventory of Laurence Donovan Docs meant that Lester Dent enjoyed a break from Doc during 1936. He wrote six, and none between August and December. During this time, Dent finally had breathing space enough to crack the more prestigious pulp markets he had long coveted. To *Argosy*, he sold three serials. For *Black Mask*, which had launched the career of Dashiell Hammett and was then featuring the work of Raymond Chandler, Dent sold the often-anthologized Oscar Sail detective stories.

When Dent got back into writing Docs in 1937, he did but five. By this time Harold Davis—by then working for the *New York Daily News*, had gotten the hang of the Dent style and turned out three of his own—including the classic *Golden Peril*, the sequel to *The Man of Bronze*. His Docs, while highly imaginative, suffered from a melodramatic flavor Davis seems to have soaked up from watching Saturday matinee serials.

While writing *The Mountain Monster* in August of that year, Davis, obviously aware of his faults as a writer, told Dent:

"Truthfully, I don't think this one is as good as the last, but there wasn't as much plot to work on. However, I do think it is okay—at least it sounds that way to me as I whip it into final shape. The first three chapters were tougher than hell to write—all menace and fear build up, without carrying so far that it lost its punch. I must have rewritten those chapters at least four times, but I think they are in good shape now. While I don't think it is better than the underground yarn (*The Living Fire Menace*), I do think it is better than the one I did just before that—the return to Central America (*The Golden Peril*)."

When World War II broke out in Europe, the demands on Davis's time—he was working the telegraph desk monitoring war dispatches—cut into his ability to turn out pulp stories regularly, leaving Dent once more in the lurch.

Ironically, the next Kenneth Robeson was one who was editing Davis's manuscripts. William G. Bogart was a mild-mannered, balding assistant editor under John Nanovic, who was anxious to break away from the nine-to-five routine and freelance.

His opportunity came when Street & Smith made a deal with the New York World's Fair to promote the World of Tomorrow, as the exposition was themed, through a Doc story. While the fairgrounds were still under construction, he, Dent, and Nanovic were given a tour of the grounds, an outline was hammered out, and *World's Fair Goblin* was the result.

When the story was accepted, an exuberant Bogart wrote Lester Dent the following:

"I guess you know how I feel about receiving the check in full payment for *World's Fair Goblin*. It was just about the greatest thing that's ever happened. Though I realized I did a rush job on the yarn, and could have done much better given the time, I had built a pile of hope on it. For it was to be the means of breaking away from the grind down at S&S and making a decent living writing."

Nevertheless, Bogart was nearly cut loose when his third Doc, "Menace," was rejected by Nanovic. Dent stepped in, did a drastic rewrite and the story appeared as *The Angry Ghost*.

Dent scolded him: "I had to do a great deal of work on this story before it was acceptable, spending fully as much time as I would spend in doing a yarn of my own. I hate to put it so bluntly, but I do not feel able to spend as much effort on putting a ghosted story in acceptable condition as I had to spend in this case—and put out the kind of money I have been paying for the ghosting. The next story will have to show a very, very great improvement or we will have to terminate our ghosting arrangement, which was based on your doing acceptable stories."

Fortunately for Bogart, his next attempt, *The Flying Goblin*, was a solid story.

William Bogart, while probably the weakest writer of those to contribute to the Doc Savage canon, nevertheless proved the most enduring. He penned a total of fourteen Doc adventures, and made up in enthusiasm what he lacked creatively. Bogart very much enjoyed writing the novels and saw the opportunity as central to his freelancing career. He was especially fond of stories in which important U.S. industries were threatened by evil forces, as exemplified by *The Angry Ghost* and

Tunnel Terror, and put a great deal of energy into visiting steel mills, Army fortifications, and other localities he would employ as story backgrounds.

When Harold Davis dropped out of fiction writing upon being chosen to help launch *Newsday* early in 1940, Bogart thought he had a clear field. Then Alan Hathway entered the picture.

Alan "Happy" Hathway was a colorful figure who as a young man ran away from Sault Sainte Marie, Michigan, and his father's lumber company, to see the world. After knocking around the Orient, he ended up in Chicago, where he became the epitome of a Roaring Twenties newspaperman.

By 1936, he was with the *Daily News,* where he met Harold Davis, who introduced him to John Nanovic. Hathway soon became another of the frequent contributors to the back pages of Nanovic's string of pulp magazines.

Like Donovan, Hathway wrote directly for Nanovic on Doc Savage which meant that Dent had neither the responsibility nor the chore of revising his manuscripts. In Hathway's case, there was no necessity. He had an uncanny knack for emulating the exuberant Dent style. His prose was also reminiscent of Davis's best work.

This was no coincidence. The pair were known to kibitz on each other's stories. It's not beyond the realm of possibility that Hathway had pitched in to help Davis on his Docs and that Davis might not have returned the favor. Ironically, Hathway's best Doc, *The Devil's Playground,* employed the Michigan lumber industry as a backdrop.

Alan Hathway wrote only four Docs because Nanovic assigned him to revive Laurence Donovan's old character, The Whisperer, for a brief run. Hathway had taken a leave of absence from the *News* to write pulp fiction exclusively. After *The Whisperer* went bellyup in 1942,

Davis took on Hathway as *Newsday*'s city editor. In 1944, Hathway replaced Davis as managing editor and went on to a stellar career with that paper, and was instrumental in winning its 1954 Pulitzer Prize, about political corruption on Long Island.

Asked about his brief pulp writing career less than a year before his death, Alan Hathway would say only, "Those days are ancient history and I'm not interested in talking about them."

The loss of Davis in 1940 left Dent hunting for another backup Robeson. He is known to have approached science fiction writer Edmond Hamilton, then writing the Doc Savage imitation, *Captain Future*. Hamilton, although flattered, had to beg off because of his workload. When that happened, Hamilton's editor, Mort Weisinger and a fellow editor, Jack Schiff—later to edit *Superman* and *Batman* comics respectively—offered to rush into the breach. They pitched a plot called "Dead Man's Club."

Unfortunately, before Dent could act on it, Street & Smith cut his pay substantially, reducing the margin which enabled him to pay his ghosts competitive rates. Slacking *Doc Savage* sales possibly signaled that readers were finding the plethora of ghosted stories a poor substitute for the "real" Kenneth Robeson. Dent wrote *Birds of Death* from the plot which he purchased from Weisinger and Schiff.

The era of the Doc Savage ghost was over—for a while, anyway.

By this time, the byline Kenneth Robeson was no longer exclusive to the Doc Savage series. Earlier, Nanovic had begun running a serial feature on Doc's exercises, called "The Doc Savage Method of Self-Development." These were bylined Kenneth Robeson, but in fact were the work of Dr. Paul Rothenberger and another Nanovic assistant, Morris Ogden Jones.

In 1939, bowing to continuing reader requests for two Doc novels a month, Nanovic did the next best thing and launched *The Avenger* magazine, which was touted as by "the Creator of Doc Savage." This was a harmless publishing fiction. In fact, the man behind the Kenneth Robeson byline on *The Avenger* was named Paul Ernst. Dent's sole contribution to the new series was to sit down with Paul Ernst, and, along with Shadow author Walter Gibson, give him the benefit of their extensive experience guiding a single character through monthly exploits. When *The Avenger* was canceled in 1942 and the character given a new home in *Clues Detective*, Emile C. Tepperman did the honors, again writing as Kenneth Robeson. (When the character was revived in the 1970s, Ron Goulart inherited the *nom de plume*.)

One little-known use of the Robeson byline was on the Ed Stone series, which ran in *Crime Busters* between 1938-1939. Lester Dent himself wrote this obscure series about a former pugilist and his Chinese valet who solved whacky mysteries.

World War II had no sooner ended when Lester Dent, having borne the monthly Doc Savage load for five straight years without a break, decided it was time to move on. He was not prepared to abandon Doc entirely however. By subcontracting the books, he could retain a portion of the payments. He contacted all of his ghosts who were still writing. Ryerson Johnson declined. Harold Davis was more than willing to give it a try, but his initial return effort, *The Exploding Lake*, was a failure which, as he had so many times before, Dent was forced to salvage in revision.

That left just Bogart, who had gone back to the working world as an advertising copywriter. With the opportunity to become the sole Kenneth Robeson dangled before him, Bogart happily quit his job and settled down to writing.

Dent had begun selling mystery novels to Doubleday's Crime Club line, and that was where he saw his future. Upon turning in *The Devil Is Jones*, in April, 1946, Dent thought he had written his last Doc Savage. But Bogart had trouble meeting deadlines so Dent pitched in with another Doc, *Danger Lies East*.

Then, Street & Smith decided to drop Doc's frequency to bi-monthly and retitle the magazine *Doc Savage Science Detective*. Dent was asked to pitch in again. Fear that if he refused the company would cut him and Bogart off, forced Dent to comply. (His fears were well-grounded. Walter Gibson and John D. MacDonald were approached as replacements. Both declined.)

As it turned out, the new schedule left no room for Bogart, who suddenly found himself without a steady writing income. His situation must have been desperate because at one point, he hastily rewrote one of his old Docs, *The Magic Forest*, and peddled it to a rival magazine under the title, *The Crazy Indian*. Although he changed all character names, in a few spots Bogart slipped up and the familiar names of Doc, Monk, and Ham actually made it into print, creating a kind of orphan Doc story.

Oddly, around this time one of Dent's former secretaries, Evelyn Coulson, contacted Dent, offering to ghost the series. She had been a writer of pulp love stories. Dent politely informed her that Bogart had the job. The letter suggests that Coulson had performed this service before, but there is no concrete record of Coulson ever having ghosted a Doc. If she had, that would make her the only distaff Kenneth Robeson of an otherwise all-male club.

After *Doc Savage* magazine was cancelled in 1949,

the house name Kenneth Robeson was retired until
Bantam Books revived the Doc series, which I'm privi-
leged to be continuing.

Most of the writers who toiled behind the Kenneth
Robeson byline are dead now. Harold A. Davis died in
1955. The date of Laurence Donovan's demise, believed
to be in the late forties, is unknown. Lester Dent, of
course, died in 1959. Both Hathway and Bogart passed
away in 1977.

Only Ryerson Johnson, still freelancing at the age
of 90, survives of the noble crew.

As for myself, the newest writer to assume the
Kenneth Robeson byline, my association with Doc Savage began in January 1969 when I picked up a Bantam
edition of *Dust of Death*, and became a lifelong fan.

My fascination with Doc led to my becoming the
literary agent for Mrs. Lester Dent, on whose behalf I
brought Lester Dent's long-unpublished Doc novel,
The Red Spider, to the attention of Bantam Books,
which published it in 1979. In 1985, I adapted one of
Lester Dent's favorite Docs, *The Thousand-Headed
Man*, as a six-part serial for National Public Radio's
Adventures of Doc Savage show. (The other serial adap-
tation, *Fear Cay*, was scripted by the show's producer/
director Roger Rittner.)

In my well-received afterword to the final Doc
Savage Omnibus, I explained the origins of my first
three Docs and expressed the hope that I would pen
more. I'm pleased to announce that Bantam Books has
asked me to write four additional Doc novels.

Next follows *The Jade Ogre*, a bloody adventure
that propels Doc Savage from 1935 San Francisco to
Hong Kong, and finally to a spider-haunted Cambodian
ruin ruled by the legendary Jade Ogre, an armless
creature with the extraordinary power to project phantom death-dealing arms to any spot on earth.

Flight into Fear is a sequel to *The Red Spider*, in which Doc Savage is marked for assassination by the Kremlin. His assassin is a mystery woman known only as the Red Widow. Inasmuch as Doc is ordinarily afraid of women, the Soviets may have picked the perfect tool with which to do away with the Man of Bronze.

The Whistling Wraith, finds Doc Savage called to Washington D.C. to help solve the disappearance of a visiting Balkan king who has mysteriously vanished from his motorcade en route to the White House. Doc's only clue is a mournful whistling overheard just before the dignitary vanished.

In *The Forgotten Realm*, Doc must solve the mystery of an escaped madman calling himself "X Man." The trail leads to the heart of the African jungle, where a dormant volcano hides a lost survival from antiquity.

In each case, these new adventures will be based upon existing Lester Dent outlines and manuscripts. *Flight into Fear* is especially noteworthy inasmuch as its source is an original unpublished Lester Dent Cold War novel, which I've rewritten for inclusion in the Doc Savage series. I've taken great pains to preserve as much of the original draft as possible.

This is as it should be, because this particular Kenneth Robeson sees his mandate as continuing in the spirit of the writer who started it all—Lester Dent.

It's also my way of making amends to Dent, who if he were here, would almost certainly castigate me for willingly writing under the house name he despised but which I consider one of the great bylines in popular fiction.

—WILL MURRAY

INDEX TO THE DOC SAVAGE NOVELS

In answer to many requests, we are including a complete index to the original Doc Savage novels as they were first presented in *Doc Savage Magazine;* and for those still trying to complete a coveted set of the Bantam Books reprints, a second index to the paperback series, along with the true authors—where known—identified.

The author listings are as complete and as accurate as they can possibly be made. No central record exists that identifies the true identities of the many Kenneth Robesons. This listing has been assembled from a collation of the original Street & Smith payment records with Lester Dent's personal files, now on deposit in the University of Missouri's Western Historical Manuscript Collection in Columbia. It may be there are other authors involved with the series, or that some of the ghost writers have not been completely credited for their work. We may never know, for instance, whether any of the stories individually credited to Harold A. Davis or Alan Hathway might not be collaborations between the two men. Or that there might not be more Davis stories that Dent so drastically rewrote that all trace of Davis's contribution has been obliterated.

In cases where a ghost writer wrote from a Lester

Dent plot or outline, and where Dent revised the manuscript of another writer, or made substantial suggestions on how a story was to be written, Dent is given co-author credit. By no means are these author attributions definitive.

Where Bantam Books has seen fit to retitle a novel, the pulp magazine title follows, set in brackets.

Street & Smith's *Doc Savage Magazine*

1)	Mar.	1933	The Man of Bronze
2)	Apr.	1933	The Land of Terror
3)	May	1933	Quest of the Spider
4)	June	1933	The Polar Treasure
5)	July	1933	Pirate of the Pacific
6)	Aug.	1933	The Red Skull
7)	Sep.	1933	The Lost Oasis
8)	Oct.	1933	The Sargasso Ogre
9)	Nov.	1933	The Czar of Fear
10)	Dec.	1933	The Phantom City
11)	Jan.	1934	Brand of the Werewolf
12)	Feb.	1934	The Man Who Shook the Earth
13)	Mar.	1934	Meteor Menace
14)	Apr.	1934	The Monsters
15)	May	1934	The Mystery on the Snow
16)	June	1934	The King Maker
17)	July	1934	The Thousand-Headed Man
18)	Aug.	1934	The Squeaking Goblin
19)	Sep.	1934	Fear Cay
20)	Oct.	1934	Death in Silver
21)	Nov.	1934	The Sea Magician
22)	Dec.	1934	The Annihilist
23)	Jan.	1935	The Mystic Mullah

58) Dec. 1937 The Golden Peril

59) Jan. 1938 The Living Fire Menace
60) Feb. 1938 The Mountain Monster
61) Mar. 1938 Devil on the Moon
62) Apr. 1938 The Pirate's Ghost
63) May   1938 The Motion Menace
64) June 1938 The Submarine Mystery
65) July 1938 The Giggling Ghosts
66) Aug. 1938 The Munitions Master
67) Sep. 1938 The Red Terrors
68) Oct. 1938 Fortress of Solitude
69) Nov. 1938 The Green Death
70) Dec. 1938 The Devil Genghis

71) Jan. 1939 Mad Mesa
72) Feb. 1939 The Yellow Cloud
73) Mar. 1939 The Freckled Shark
74) Apr. 1939 World's Fair Goblin
75) May   1939 The Gold Ogre
76) June 1939 The Flaming Falcons
77) July 1939 Merchants of Disaster
78) Aug. 1939 The Crimson Serpent
79) Sep. 1939 Poison Island
80) Oct. 1939 The Stone Man
81) Nov. 1939 Hex
82) Dec. 1939 The Dagger in the Sky

83) Jan. 1940 The Other World
84) Feb. 1940 The Angry Ghost
85) Mar. 1940 The Spotted Men
86) Apr. 1940 The Evil Gnome
87) May   1940 The Boss of Terror
88) June 1940 The Awful Egg
89) July 1940 The Flying Goblin
90) Aug. 1940 Tunnel Terror

124) June	1943	The Running Skeletons
125) July	1943	Mystery on Happy Bones
126) Aug.	1943	The Mental Monster
127) Sep.	1943	Hell Below
128) Oct.	1943	The Goblins
129) Nov.	1943	The Secret of the Su
130) Dec.	1943	The Spook of Grandpa Eben
131) Jan.	1944	According to Plan of a One-Eyed Mystic
132) Feb.	1944	Death Had Yellow Eyes
133) Mar.	1944	The Derelict of Skull Shoal
134) Apr.	1944	The Whisker of Hercules
135) May	1944	The Three Devils
136) June	1944	The Pharaoh's Ghost
137) July	1944	The Man Who Was Scared
138) Aug.	1944	The Shape of Terror
139) Sep.	1944	Weird Valley
140) Oct.	1944	Jiu San
141) Nov.	1944	Satan Black
142) Dec.	1944	The Lost Giant
143) Jan.	1945	Violent Night
144) Feb.	1945	Strange Fish
145) Mar.	1945	The Ten-Ton Snakes
146) Apr.	1945	Cargo Unknown
147) May	1945	Rock Sinister
148) June	1945	The Terrible Stork
149) July	1945	King Joe Cay
150) Aug.	1945	The Wee Ones
151) Sep.	1945	Terror Takes 7
152) Oct.	1945	The Thing That Pursued
153) Nov.	1945	Trouble on Parade
154) Dec.	1945	The Screaming Man
155) Jan.	1946	Measures for a Coffin

Unpublished in magazine form:

The Bantam Books Doc Savage Series

1)	The Man of Bronze	Lester Dent
2)	The Thousand-Headed Man	"
3)	Meteor Menace	"
4)	The Polar Treasure	"
5)	Brand of the Werewolf	"
6)	The Lost Oasis	"
7)	The Monsters	"
8)	The Land of Terror	"
9)	The Mystic Mullah	"
10)	The Phantom City	"
11)	Fear Cay	"
12)	Quest of Qui	"
13)	Land of Always-Night	W. Ryerson Johnson & Lester Dent
14)	The Fantastic Island	"
15)	Murder Melody	Laurence Donovan
16)	The Spook Legion	Lester Dent
17)	The Red Skull	"
18)	The Sargasso Ogre	"
19)	Pirate of the Pacific	"
20)	The Secret in the Sky	"
21)	Cold Death	Laurence Donovan
22)	The Czar of Fear	Lester Dent
23)	Fortress of Solitude	"
24)	The Green Eagle	"
25)	The Devil's Playground	Alan Hathway
26)	Death in Silver	Lester Dent
27)	Mystery Under the Sea	"
28)	The Deadly Dwarf [Repel]	"
29)	The Other World	"
30)	The Flaming Falcons	"
31)	The Annihilist	"
32)	Dust of Death	Harold A. Davis & Lester Dent
33)	The Terror in the Navy	Lester Dent

Beginning with the edition numbered #97-98, Bantam Books began reprinting two novels in one volume:

Beginning with reprint #127, Bantam began collecting multiple novels in single omnibus volumes, and numbering by volume rather than title.

DOC SAVAGE OMNIBUS #1

DOC SAVAGE OMNIBUS #2

DOC SAVAGE OMNIBUS #3

DOC SAVAGE OMNIBUS #4

DOC SAVAGE OMNIBUS #5

DOC SAVAGE OMNIBUS #6

Continue the all-new series written by Will Murray, writing as Kenneth Robeson, with an adventure story based on an unpublished outline written by Lester Dent. This yarn begins in the fog-shrouded byways of San Francisco where clutching, ghostly hands seek any who oppose . . .

THE JADE OGRE

A desperate plea for help plunged Doc Savage into a maelstrom of horror aboard the Hongkong-bound liner, **Mandarin**, where the depraved minions of the phantom predator, Quon, hold sway. As innocent passengers succumb to the insidious Jade Fever, and ghost-green hands pursue Doc's beautiful cousin, Patricia, the mighty Man of Bronze races to solve a riddle that defies reason.

For deep in the spider-haunted ruins of far-away Cambodia brooks a twisted, armless creature with a face of jade—The Jade Ogre—whose power to project deadly, disembodied arms to any place on earth makes him the most dangerous foe Doc Savage has ever faced. And who lives to annihilate all lesser mortals!

Here is the exciting first-chapter preview from *THE JADE OGRE*.

San Francisco is a city of fogs.

From the first sultry breeze of Spring to the dwindling days of the Fall season, the cottony stuff pours in through the Golden Gate like ghostly combers, to wash over San Francisco Bay and envelope the peninsula on which the metropolis reposes.

Unlike those of London, another famous fog-bound city, the fogs of San Francisco are not stagnant masses of moisture having the consistency of pea soup. On certain days they do lumber in like a damp, prowling animal to deposit a clammy residue on all they touch. Meteorologists call these mists, wet fogs. There is also a species of stratus—another word for fog—known as dry fog. In contrast to the wet variety, the dry fog is smooth as tobacco smoke and as silky as spider silk. It is not as unpleasant to wander through, though it is every bit as impenetrable to sight.

On this day, the fog that enwrapped the hills of San Francisco was of the dry variety. It had formed close off-shore and prowled inland without opportunity to collect ocean moisture—thus its dry quality.

It lacked but an hour to sunset, so the fog was not unpleasantly dreary. In fact, it was rather bright. A poet—and San Francisco had no shortage of these—might have dubbed it "white murk." It had settled low upon the city so that only its many precipitous hills poked up to receive the sun, giving the metropolis a fantastical aspect, like an archipelago in a sea of haze.

A man shoved through this vaporous atmosphere. He was a squat, powerful individual, possessing a belligerent strut somewhat remindful of a bulldog. An expensive gabardine coat strained to contain his rolling shoulders, collar pulled up to his ears to fend off a late Spring chill. The brim of a tasteful soft hat was yanked down lower than good taste would ordinarily permit.

As he walked, the man clutched a cloth hand bag, which he held close to his body—close so that it was not obvious that the bag was manacled to his wrist with steel handcuffs that had been deliberately soiled so they would not catch the light.

The fog was thick. It was impossible to see more than a half dozen feet beyond one's nose. Yet the man strode along as if the opalescent atmosphere was as transparent as glass. The spectral stuff seemed to swallow the sound of his heavy shoes as they tramped along the worn cobbles.

The din of the city—clangings of streetcars and the ceaseless foghorns and ferry blasts from out on the bay—might have explained the seeming silence of the man's progress.

Often, the man paused, cocking his head to one side, as if listening. He evidently detected no sounds other than the normal clamour of civilization, for each time he proceeded as before.

The man seemed to have a specific destination in mind. He deviated from his path only once. And that was when his nostrils wrinkled up at the spicy tang emanating from a part of the city where neon lights threw vermillion and emerald glare into the low-hanging puddle of fog.

The man stopped, hesitated and muttered a single word to himself.

"Chinatown."

Under the yanked-down hatbrim, his dark eyes narrowed.

Abruptly, he barrelled across a busy street, dodging a whining taxi cab, went south three blocks, then east two.

He paused often, listening. And hearing nothing he deemed out of the ordinary, continued on.

At the foot of steep California Street, the bundled-up bulldog of a man paused outside a drug store, before which a streetcar was being turned. Some trick of atmospheric turbulence created a zone of clear air around the bulky car.

Evidently intrigued, the wanderer stood watching as the streetcar—which had just disgorged its allotment of passengers—was turned about on a circular track. Several men did this by pushing and shoving the car by hand—a knot of them pushing the front one way and the back the other—until the flat nose of the car was pointing back up the hill. They had to put their backs into it.

The conductor jangled the bell, adding to the ceaseless din. Passengers—among them a number of those who assisted the strenuous turnabout maneuver—climbed aboard.

But the loitering bulldog of a man had by that time lost interest in the proceedings. His eyes scanned the surrounding white blanket of vapor which was slowly reclaiming the zone of clarity. He fingered an ear forward.

Then he slipped into the drugstore, whose sign proclaimed it to be the Wise Owl Drugstore. The owl seemed to blink its eyes every so many seconds—an illusion accomplished by the simple action of two light bulbs timed to wink on and off at intervals.

At a pay phone, the man made a terse telephone call.

"Hello? Connect me with San Francisco Municipal Airport."

After a pause, he asked, "Is the *Solar Speedster* still due in at nine o'clock? You say it will be a half hour late? Thank you."

He dropped another nickel into the slot and requested the steamship pier.

This time, he spoke in low tones, such as would thwart an eavesdropper, should any be lurking near by. Evidently, the other party had difficulty understanding his speech. He was forced to repeat himself.

"I asked if my luggage had been put aboard," he said, testily. "The *Mandarin*. She sails in the morning."

Upon being assured that all was well, the man in gabardine left the booth with his face—what could be seen of it—screwed up into an unhappy knot, and silently purchased a package of gum at the counter.

He paused under the bright winking eyes of the electric owl, peeling the tinfoil off a stick of gum with a practiced one-handed maneuver. He shoved it into his mouth, and began masticating it thoughtfully, his eyes and ears alert. He sniffed the air surreptitiously.

Satisfied that he was not being shadowed, the man in the gabardine coat resumed his eastward progress.

"Blast this fog," he muttered.

The man had not ventured seven blocks when he passed an alley that was like a fallen cracker box stuffed with smoke. As if scenting an unpleasant odor, his nose wrinkled up as he passed it. Bulldog-like, he bared his teeth in a grimace. The man quickened his pace.

At the next corner, he sidestepped onto the cross street and set his broad back to a brick wall. Spitting out his gum, his free hand—it was his right—fumbled the buttons of his gabardine coat open, snaked in, and withdrew a single cigarette, which oddly enough, he crushed and placed in his mouth.

He began to chew furiously.

Then hand went back into his garment and came out again filled with a big revolver.

It was a .45, the barrel bulldogged off until it was less

than an inch in length. The thing was capable of blowing a young posthole through a man's innards.

The man set himself. His jaws ceased their animated chewing. Oddly, he sniffed the air like a hound, as if not trusting his other senses, which in the muffling fog, might have been wise.

As if stepping from another plane of existence, a figure emerged from the bulwark of fog.

He was a Chinese. The way his slanted orbs narrowed made that clear. Otherwise, he was dressed as any other inhabitant of San Francisco. The days of the pigtail and the colorful brocaded silk jacket are long past.

The Celestial possessed a wizened body surmounted by a face that was as yellow and wrinkled as a dried tangerine. In one shriveled claw, he clutched a red rubber sponge. From the other dangled a loop of scarlet cord, apparently of silk.

"Strangler, eh?" growled the man in gabardine.

At that, the wizened individual jumped as if snake-bit. His narrowed eyes flew wide as he whirled toward the unexpected sound.

And received in his eyes a squirt of saliva mixed with tobacco juice.

The fellow made a squeaking sound, sprang backward. The fog immediately swallowed him up.

In a blind attempt to brain the wizened one, the man in the gabardine coat swung his hand bag into the fog. The bag connected. It brought a high-pitched yelp of pain.

"What's the matter, Chinaman? Can't take it?"

The Celestial lunged from the fog. He had lost his sponge, but the red silken cord now stretched taunt between two lemon-colored claws.

"I no strangle you," he snarled. It was an absurd denial under the circumstances. The Oriental blinked and squinted as the painful tobacco juice seared his slant eyes.

"No?" said the other. "Then you won't be needing *this!*"

The bulldogged revolver barrel swept up, the gun sight hooking the taut silken noose. The latter snarled as it parted, leaving two ragged ends hanging useless from too-tight fists.

Suddenly bereft of his tool of murder, the Celestial closed in, holding one smarting orb open with bony fingers. He kicked out.

The waylayer in gabardine grabbed the foot before it could connect. He used his left hand. The heavy hand bag swung free from his manacled wrist, making a heavy clicking sound like the action of the tumblers of a combination safe.

The kick had been a bit of Oriental trickery. The Chinaman flipped his free hand out and accomplished his purpose—settled one fragment of the noose of red silk about the other's thick neck. The silk had been unusually long.

The man in gabardine turtled his head down inside his burly shoulders. Throat muscles like ropes tightened against the garrot cord. Still holding the Chinese by the ankles, he struggled to point the stubby revolver in a useful direction, but the Celestial cannily slipped around behind him.

The noose tightened further, bringing a grunt of pain welling up from the man's throat.

He reacted to this by levering with the hand that clamped the Celestial's ankle. The Oriental squawled in agony, producing a sound such as a grass blade makes when it is blown between the hands.

There was not much flesh over the Celestial's ankle bones and the pop as they broke produced a distinct report.

The Chinaman made more squawling noises. He flung his spindly weight on the garrot cord. It cut through the resistance of the struggling man's neck muscles, plugging his straining windpipe.

Convulsively, the man who was struggling to avoid strangulation lifted his revolver straight up and fired twice. The sound was loud. But it seemed to become lost in the incessant tooting of foghorns and squeal of passing streetcars.

The Oriental was fighting like a crippled rat. His opponent swung a foot and kicked the yellow man's remaining leg from under him, but the jerk as the fellow fell only set the garrot cord deeper into flesh.

The victim's face was reddening. Sweat streamed down his nose. He lost his hat, exposing rough, muscular features and sweat-plastered blondish hair.

Grunting and scraping his feet, the man finally succeeded in dragging his would-be throttler to the grimey face of the corner brick wall. The strangler, intent upon his strenuous work, was pulled along in spite of himself.

When he heard the click of his sawed-off gun muzzle against brick, the man in gabardine gave a mighty grunt and swung his thick body around—sending the Chinaman hopping into the wall.

The Celestial bleated in pain. His grip loosened a moment. A moment was all that was necessary. Inhaling a sobbing gulp of air, the man in gabardine threw himself into the energetic task of slamming his muscular body into the wall repeatedly.

The unfortunate Chinese, caught between the human wall and the one of brick, was pummeled into submission in this fashion. His fingers let go of the red silken strangling cord. Left with only one good leg for support, he sat down hard.

"Who sent you?" grated the man in gabardine, towering over the other.

"I lefuse to say," the beaten Oriental singsonged stubbornly.

"Wan Sop?"

The waylayer's bloodied lips thinned.

"Quon?"

"I know not that name," the waylayer who had been waylaid mumbled evasively. His eyes were squeezed tight, squinting against the sting of tobacco juice.

"Liar," said the man in gabardine, who promptly knocked the Chinese unconscious with the stubby muzzle of his weapon. But only after breaking open the cylinder and removing the bullets with the same practiced one-handed manipulation that told he was used to operating with his left hand manacled to the cloth hand bag.

The Chinese made no sound. He simply went slack where he sat. His ratlike chin came to rest in his coat front and his breathing became noisy.

Pocketing his revolver, the man in gabardine got down on his hands and knees and felt around the pavement for the dropped garrotte. He cursed the low-lying fog, which swallowed his groping hands to the wrists as if they had disappeared into another realm of existence.

He soon found both torn ends, along with the red rubber sponge. Ripping the cord into a third length, he bound the insensate Celestial's wrists and ankles with expert skill. Lifting the man's head by his coarse black hair, he popped the sponge into the gaping mouth whose teeth were red-black with the staining that comes from a life of chewing betel nuts.

Finally, he tied the sponge in place with the shortest length of silk. He stood up.

"Give my regards to Wan Sop when you wake up, Chinaman," spat the man in gabardine just before he melted into the smoky silk of the afternoon fog, rubbing his chafed raw throat.

A witness—and there were none—might have noted that the man in gabardine retraced his path, returning the way he had come. His progress was as before—except that he took pains to give Chinatown a wider berth on the return walk.

A little less than twenty minutes later, the same man was inserting a key into an aperture below a frosted glass door panel. The key grated the lock mechanism into submission, and the man shoved in, using one thick shoulder for that purpose. He kicked the door shut with the heel of his shoe, his free hand simultaneously sweeping upwards toward a wall light switch. The door banged shut.

In the darkness, he froze, his nose wrinkling with evident distaste.

"Damn," he muttered. Then, more loudly, he said. "I know some one is in here."

"You must have eyes like cat," a singsong voice intoned.

"No, but I recognize the stink of joss house incense when it tickles my nose," the man grunted. "And this room reeks of it."

"Since surprise has been lost to us all, you need not delay turning on light."

The man completed his gesture. Light flooded the reception area of a mid-sized office suite, disclosing a gaggle of lemon-skinned individuals.

They wore the raiment of modern civilization, but their placid, almond-eyed countenances bespoke the Orient. There were five of them, and as the man in gabardine took them in with hard, unflinching eyes, his gaze went to one in particular, who stood out from the rest by virtue of the saffron quality of his complexion. The others ran more to brown.

"*Hao jui mei jian*," hissed the voice that had spoken from the darkness.

"Speak English, dammit!"

"I said, 'Long time no see,'" stated the calm voice. "Jason Baild."

"It's Baird, you damned rice-eating footpad," spat the one addressed as Jason Baird. "And I happen to know you speak English as well as any one."

"I prefer to be addressed by my honorable name," said the Celestial, his dark eyes glittering with menace. He was slender, emaciated, with a gnarled yellow rope for a neck and a head that was like an old skull that had been stuccoed with lemon peel. His teeth were big, the lips were so thin the shape of his teeth showed through. His eyes were remindful of dirty clay marbles in his fleshless skull, and his pate was perfectly hairless.

"There's nothing honorable about it," snarled the man who was evidently Jason Baird, proprietor of Gold Coast Lapidary. "*Wan Sop.*"

"And there is nothing wise in your attempts to thwart the will of Quon," retorted Wan Sop. "In fact, it is very foolish of you to do so. You see, we know that you have enlisted aid in your cause."

"Then you know what you are up against," Baird countered.

Wan Sop shrugged unconcernedly. "We do not fear a mere mortal, no matter how formidable his reputation, for we serve one whose power is beyond challenge, and whose jade breath is as inescapable as fate."

Jason Baird's lips writhed in a humorless grin. "Bunk."

"You will come to fear the searing touch of our illustrious master," asserted skull-headed Wan Sop. He cackled something in an unintelligible lingo.

Wan Sop's satellites started forward.

Jason Baird lifted his right hand toward his open coat front.

"*Hul soung!*" Wan Sop shrilled. "Watch out! He has gun!"

The bulldogged revolver never emerged, however.

A brown-skinned Asiatic made an up-and-under motion like a man pitching a horseshoe. It could be seen that the sleeve of the man's modern business coat was cut wide in the Oriental fashion. Something slashed from within. The space between his suddenly outflung fingers and Jason Baird whizzed like a typewriter carriage returning.

Something struck Baird in the precise center of his forehead. With an explosive grunt, he fell forward—a dragon-hilted dagger clattering on the bare floor by his crumpling figure. It had emerged from one of the ridiculously wide sleeves—no longer quite so ridiculous now that its true purpose was revealed.

"*Ho ho,*" said Wan Sop, eyeing the sprawled figure that was Jason Baird. "Very Good. You are a true servant of the Armless One, Sing Fat."

"*Dor ja,*" said the one addressed as Sing Fat, in the manner of a person acknowledging a flowery compliment. "I strive for worthiness before the inscrutable jade visage of He Who Will Breathe Death Upon The Universe."

Wan Sop advanced on the sprawled figure, who gave out a groan when kicked.

"Such a foolish one," he chuckled. "Strip him, O limbs of the Jade Ogre."

The satellites of Wan Sop fell to their knees and rolled insensate Jason Baird onto his back. They began picking apart his clothing, insinuating spidery fingers into pockets and turning them inside out. Contents were examined. A fat billfold was offered to Wan Sop, who, after a careful examination of its contents, pocketed it.

"Nothing, *Sin Song*," said a man respectfully. *Sin Song* was evidently some form of address akin to master.

"Remove his shoes," directed Wan Sop.

At that, Jason Baird began kicking furiously. An Asiatic picked up the dragon-shaped dagger and lay the wavy edge of it against Jason Baird's throat. The burly bulldog of a jeweler subsided.

His shoes were swiftly unlaced and his stockings removed.

Wan Sop leaned down to examine the bare soles of Jason Baird's feet. The jeweler began kicking anew. Yellow and brown hands were laid across his ankles, pinpointing them.

"A thousand pardons," said Wan Sop, and then dug two curved finger nails into the leathery hide that was the sole of Jason Baird's left foot.

The nails seemed to penetrate the flesh. Sharp points actually disappeared from view. Strangely, no blood seeped.

With a vicious yank that brought a yelp from Baird's lips, Wan Sop reclaimed his finger nails. A ripping sound accompanied this grisly procedure. Jason Baird threshed and howled, as if in excruciating pain. The Orientals displayed fierce grins as if enjoying the torture being inflicted upon the jeweler.

Grinning, Wan Sop brought to light a curling swatch of what seemed to be raw flesh. He allowed this to twirl in the light, showing it to be merely flesh-colored adhesive tape, to which he affixed a folded square of paper.

The bare sole of Jason Baird evinced no injury.

Delicately, Wan Sop pulled the paper free, discarding the flesh-colored tape into a nearby waste paper basket. The paper unfolded under his careful fingers. A small silvery key fell out. Nimble yellow finger flashed out, cupping it before it fell to the floor.

"Your ways are known to us, Jason Baird," intoned Wan Sop. "This item is meant for others, should an unfortunate fate overtake your worthy personage."

"You go to hell, heathen," spat Jason Baird.

Wan Sop pointedly declined to answer this invitation. His gray almond-shaped eyes were on the paper. They narrowed as they absorbed the words scrawled thereon.

"Perhaps you are more clever than we supposed," enunciated Wan Sop slowly.

"Just catching on to that, are you?" Jason Baird retorted hotly.

Just then, a shadow appeared at the frosted panel of the office door.

Wide-sleeved jacket sleeves shivered as ornate daggers were shook from placed of concealment and into waiting hands. Lean bodies tensed expectantly.

"Wait," hissed Wan Sop. "It is Seed."

A hand reached for the door knob, yanked it open.

In the sudden wash of light, a man was framed. He was a white man, but his furtive air proclaimed him to be a confederate of the group of Celestials that had gathered in the office suite for the purpose of waylaying its owner, Jason Baird. He was short, spindly and as dried-up as his namesake.

"Enter—quickly," ordered Wan Sop.

The man addressed as Seed scurried in. The door closed. He glanced down at the prostrate form of Jason Baird.

"I see you glommed him," he muttered.

"No thanks to your illustrious person," said Wan Sop, his tone tinged with irony.

"I pulled my weight," Seed said defensively. "It was that damned Fung."

Wan Sop frowned like an evil moon. "What of Fung?"

"I found him in an alley all trussed up like a Christmas turkey," explained the one called Seed. "He was supposed to grab this bird Baird at a certain corner. I was to distract him by cadging a cigarette, while Fung got him from behind. But neither showed. So I went huntin'. Fung's still in that alley, colder than a mackerel."

Low voice mutter raced around the room. A foot reared back as if to kick helpless Jason Baird in the ribs. The blow never landed. A warning hiss from skull-visaged Wan Sop put a stop to that.

"No. He must be made to talk first."

"Do your worst, heathen," spat Jason Baird. "I've nothing to say to you or your yellow cut-throats."

"I wish very little from you," purred Wan Sop. "Merely the time and place of your rendezvous with the bronze man, Doc Savage."

At the enunciation of the name Doc Savage, a hush fell over the office suite. The satellites of Wan Sop seemed to lose all animation, to become standing Buddhas bereft of all menace and confidence. Their crafty eyes became catlike slits. Here and there, a pale tongue emerged to worried thin bitter lips.

Only the one called Seed displayed any outward emotion.

"Hell's bells!" he said bitterly. "Is Savage involved in this?"

"Not as yet," said Wan Sop, his soiled eyes going to the face of the man called Seed. He passed the note excavated from the sole of Jason Baird.

Seed read it, paled.

"Does this portent bother you?" inquired Wan Sop.

"Bother me?" Seed snorted. "I'll tell any man! Savage is the original trouble-buster. Birds who cross his path always come to grief."

"And those who challenge the might of the Jade Ogre," asserted Wan Sop, "spend the afterlife being pursued by phantom talons whose touch means terrible agony. This Doc Savage will be no different. You will see."

Seed twisted unwashed fingers nervously. "Maybe," he said. "But if it's all the same to you, when Savage mixes into this little affair of yours, I'll just hie myself to parts south. Like Mexico."

"Fool!" barked Wan Sop. "You cannot quit the Jade Ogre. You have been chosen to serve him, and serve him you shall."

"Well, I don't like it. I don't like it one damn little bit!"

"That is of no moment. We have a task before us." Wan Sop cast his narrow eyes down at the unfortunate face of Jason Baird. "You will not reveal what you know?"

"Never," the other gritted.

"Then you shall be made to do so at a place where resistance to the Jade Ogre is impossible. After that"—Wan Sop shrugged unconcernedly—"your destiny is unavoidable."

From a voluminous sleeve, skull-face Wan Sop produced a hypodermic whose needle was tipped by a protective bit of cork. He pulled this free, thumbed the plunger until a thin stream of bilious liquid drooled forth and knelt down to empty the contents into the wrist of Jason Baird at a point near the manacle circlet.

It took all six men to hold the husky jeweler down while this was accomplished. They retained their grips until long moments after the jeweler had ceased to twitch and strain. His breathing became shallow. Then, relaxation seized his muscular limbs.

"It is done," pronounced a sibilant singsong voice.

"It is the will of He Whose Breath Is Death," said Wan Sop solemnly.

"I still don't like this," muttered Seed uneasily. "Savage is poison."

Ignoring the complaint, skull-faced Wan Sop employed the key which had been cunningly affixed to the sole of Jason Baird's naked foot to click open the handcuffs manacling the black hand bag to the jeweler's wrist.

The Celestial shook the bag experimentally. It was heavy for its small size. The contents shook and rattled like children's play marbles.

"What do you suppose is in it?" wondered Seed, licking his thin lips. "Jewels?"

"I do not know," said Wan Sop slowly. "And there is but one key upon Baird's person.

"Seed shrugged. "Tough."

Wan Sop regarded the locked bag for several moments fixedly. His crafty eyes went to the handcuff key. On an impulse, he inserted it into the hand bag lock. It turned. The metal mouth of the bag popped open like toothless jaws.

"He is very clever, this man Baird," murmured Wan Sop, taking the open bag to the nearby desk and scattering the contents on the well-used blotter.

A scintilla of light seemed to catch the overhead light and shout back brilliance.

A collective gasp came from the lips of the assembled ruffians—with the sole exception of the contemplative Wan Sop.

"Diamonds!" Seed breathed. "Worth a small fortune, I'll bet."

Wan Sop emitted a tittering laugh. "A mere drop in bucket compared to the wealth that lies before us."

Seed shuddered involuntarily. "This business is no good," he grumbled. "I can't stand thinkin' about it. All them people gonna die."

"Think of your share, Seed," remonstrated Wan Sop. "Fix it in your mind and your conscience will trouble your days no more, and your slumber not at all."

"That don't mean I gotta like it," Seed returned, shuffling uneasily. "It's different for you China boys. I may be bad, but I'm still white. It's my kinda people who are gonna die when this thing picks up steam."

Wan Sop looked away from the scatter of diamond stones. His eyes were thin slits that might have been made by the action of a knife blade across his puffy closed eyelids.

"The imagination is no friend to the industrious," he said pointedly.

"I don't follow that," Seed mumbled, his eyes shifting to the cluster of Celestials who regarded him in impassive silence.

"I believe in your tongue this item of wisdom could be rendered as 'idle hands are the devil's friend,'" explained Wan Sop.

"Eh?"

"You will go and obtain a fitting vehicle for the removal of this troublesome one," added Wan Sop without answering. "There is much to be done now that this obstacle to the great plan of the Jade Ogre is about to be removed."

"Have it your way," Seed mumbled, shuffling out the door.

After he had departed, Wan Sop carefully scooped up the diamonds and returned them to the black bag. His satellites watched this operation with sullen inscrutability. It was plain that their chief had no thought of dividing the spoils among his henchmen.

Outside a bank of windows, the foghorns mourned the passing of day. Ferries hooted like frightened owls. And the fog pressed against the window glass in a way that made it seem as if the office buildings were packed in cotton.

When the last cold brilliant had dropped into its receptacle, Wan Sop said, "The tool known as Seed is a sword whose edge has been dulled and chipped by many battles. Such a one can only bring misfortune. He will have to be eliminated."

"It is the will of the Jade Ogre," several Orientals singsonged.

THE LEGENDARY MAN OF BRONZE—IN A THRILLING NEW ADVENTURE SERIES!

DOC SAVAGE